The Hag Rider

Thomas Fenske

A Wings ePress, Inc.
A Literary Fiction Novel

ings
ress, Inc.

Wings ePress, Inc.

Edited by: Rebecca Smith
Copy Edited by: Jeanne Smith
Executive Editor: Jeanne Smith
Cover Artist: Trishs FitzGerald-Jung

All rights reserved

Wings ePress Books
www.wingsepress.com

Copyright © 2020 by: Thomas Fenske
ISBN-13: 978-1-61309-577-5
ISBN-10: 1-61309-577-5

Published In the United States Of America

Wings ePress Inc.
3000 N. Rock Road
Newton, KS   67114

What They Are Saying About
The Hag Rider

"Fenske writes a tight tale with believable protagonists, even those questionable beings who aren't really there. The Hag Vanita reminds me at times of my Mom—always with the advice and the "I told you so" when you don't heed it—and the Civil War-era details are well researched and correct."

—Bonnie Reed Fry, consummate GoodReads.com
book reviewer (over 2700 reviews)

"*The Hag Rider* demonstrates Thomas Fenske's ability to capture an era, create a world and bring his readers into the pages as each scene comes to life, and just maybe, a truer sense of reality is uncovered. We tend to forget that soldiers are real people with families, who have known both good and bad times, but then have followed their hearts and stood by their countrymen, perhaps not even truly understanding what they were fighting for."

—Diane Bylo, co-owner of TomeTender Book Blog
(over 6300 reviews)

"I love that Fenske could bring the sentiments of the times to life, and how he offers plausible motivations. His characters are real people with nuanced views, and I root for Jack the whole time..."

—Kristen Houlihan, independent editor and
owner of The Edifying Word Book Blog

"A captivating fictional book for teens and adults that touches on history, but not in a 'history lesson' kind of way. The characters are well developed and relatable, making for an enjoyable and interesting read."

—Marianne Reese, book blogger and
author of *Skylar Moon.*

"I enjoyed this first-person account of a young man who runs away from a violent, hard-drinking father and joins up to fight in the Civil War. His kindness to a slave pays off in many ways, including an encounter with an old woman who offers him supernatural protection in the form of a little bag he carries with him. A short, entertaining read."

—Peter Guzzardi, independent editor
and author of *Emeralds of Oz*

Dedication

This book is dedicated to the bravest person I know, my wife,
Gretchen, and to all breast cancer survivors like her.

No One Fights Alone!

* * *

Acknowledgment

I want to thank several people for their wonderful insight and help as I completed *The Hag Rider*. Ginger Millican, Marianne Reese, Theresa Krogh, Debra Ferguson, and Roman Simmons all contributed a great deal to the finished product.

One

I've been called Jack as far back as I can remember, but my given name is really John. If you hang Benson on the end of that, you'll have my whole name: John Benson. I don't know much about writing down my thoughts, but a lot of things have happened since I first joined the cavalry at the tender age of fifteen. I fought in some battles and skirmishes. Got captured and taken far across the country as a prisoner. Then, when I was released, I made it all the way back home. I'm fairly certain I was a good soldier.

Now that the war is finally over and our country is trying to patch itself up, I reckon my story needs to be added to all the other stories that will no doubt be bandied about. I'd be the first to tell you I was just a small part of the entire affair. A watchmaker would call me a small cog in the workings of something a mite bigger. But I'll wager no one else has a stranger tale, and that's why I think it needs to be told. There were many mysterious things working on me that I don't understand and likely never will. I'm hoping writing down my account will help me figure some of them out. Now is the time to do it, while events are still fresh in my mind and, since nobody else is going to do it for me, I guess I'm the best man for the job.

When I was twelve years old, my mother caught an illness and soon died. One week she was as bright and shining as a full moon and the next week she was dead.

I still remember Pa running out to fetch the doctor and overhearing that dreaded and terrible word whispered on the front porch.

"Consumption," the doc had said. "There was nothing I could do."

It was like the wind had been taken out of my sails. I mean, death was not an uncommon thing. I guess you could say it was part of life. You just hoped it didn't happen to you or one of yours. The grief of it all seemed to break Pa and sparked a renewed onslaught of drinking. Without the soothing protection of my mother, I was the sole recipient of his drunken wrath. It was almost unbearable.

At the time when goods were unloaded from the big ships in Galveston, smaller steamers would make runs up the Buffalo Bayou to the nearby town of Houston. The lure of adventure seemed to ride on the hulls of these boats and I made friends with some of these captains. If the water was up, I would occasionally catch a ride. These trips usually took most of the day, up and back. The timetable of the voyage was always a tricky business, because shifting sandbars would sometimes ground the ships and cause delays. I wasn't supposed to do this without asking, but it didn't much matter whether I asked or not, because either way I knew a beating would result if I was late in returning.

One foggy night, the boat was returning from such a trip and we were very late. I had been sitting in the bow with a wrinkled old slave woman owned by a farmer named Pickell, who was also on the ship. She kept me company in the darkness, telling me crazy tales involving spirits and other things I didn't quite understand.

"Now, this here dog ghost was full of goodness, just likes they is in true life," she said. "When that boy found himself lost in them woods with the wolves stalking him, he saw dat dog ghost and followed him out the right path to his home. When he saw the candle his mother lit in the window, the ghost vanished and the boy knew he was safe again."

Her name was Vanita. She had white hair and a milky-eye that seemed to stare right through a person. Her voice was a mix of comfort and terror as she spun her yarns. I had seen her on the streets of Galveston with her master. I remembered the eye most of all. Its stare had caught my gaze one day when Pa had accosted me down near the docks. I remember her standing and watching us as he dragged me down the street.

When Vanita finished her story, the night was inky black and she could tell I was uneasy. I wasn't afraid of the dark, I was fearful of what was waiting for me when I got home, but she reassured me just the same.

"Now, now, Jack, there's never going to be no need to be afeared when Vanita is with you," she said, patting the back of my hands. "As long as there is a breath in me, I'll do my best to keeps you safe." Her words were oddly soothing.

"You see this here?" She showed me the palm of her right hand. It had deep scars cut into it in the form of two V shapes.

"What happened to you?"

"When I was just a young girl, my massah done cuts them two letters from my name into my palm as punishment for sassing him. I always spoke my mind, even as a child. It pained me something awful. The remembrance of that pain helps me even now. I swore then I'd protect and give people what aid I can as best as I can. You remember what you're seeing and you'll know I mean what I say."

Pa was waiting on the dock when we eased in and tied up. I could smell the booze on him even before we stopped moving. I jumped down to the dock.

"Boy! How dare you do this to me!"

I shied away from him as he raised a fist, but as soon as he did, a high-pitched shriek pierced the darkness.

"Don't you dare touch that boy!"

Tiny Vanita peered down at us from the bow, her white hair framing her head from under her kerchief like a halo. Her milky eye seemed to be shining like a beacon of light. She might have seemed to be a shriveled old woman, but she looked eight feet tall standing above the dock.

I don't know if her eye cut through to Pa's soul like it did to me, but he stopped and stared up at her and I swear I thought I felt the hand holding my shirt begin to tremble.

"Go away, you old hag. This ain't no business of yours."

About that time old man Pickell came running up. Pa had taken a step toward the boat and Pickell interceded. "Vanita Valine, what do you mean raising your voice to a white man?"

"Slave or no slave, I ain't going to stand by when a man's about to thrash a young boy for no other reason than he's drunk hisself stupid."

She turned her head toward her master and even he paused at the sight of the cold gaze of that white eye. Pickell looked over at Pa and me, and I looked up at Pa, who was wide-eyed and sweating.

He lowered his fist and turned away, taking me by the shoulder. "Git on home now." His voice had taken a calmer tone.

After we turned a dark corner and were out of sight from the ship, he whacked me good on the back of my head.

"Vanita Valine! How could you be so stupid as to consort with a witch woman? You stay clear of her, you hear? Everybody knows she's a hoodoo trick doctor and hag rider. She'll grab your soul from you. Chew you up and spit you out."

I knew better than to say anything more. There was something in his voice that told me she had scared him even more than I could understand at the time. I didn't know anything about her being a witch. She had been nice to me and just kept me company on the trip.

Oh, and she told me I didn't need to be afraid when she was with me.

Two

Pa didn't beat me that night, but he continued to drink, and whenever he drank, there was a good chance I'd have a raised fist to look forward to. It never seemed to matter what I had done; it was never the right thing in his bloodshot eyes. I was big for my age, and getting stronger, but I was still no match for him. Besides, he was my pa, and I didn't much want to fight with him.

I'd taken to having many odd and vivid dreams. I'd never been much prone to dreaming, but ever since the night on the dock, these dreams had been a part of me.

Pa was out late one night. I'd done my chores as perfect as I knew how, but I knew he'd find something wrong with one of them. I also knew that the later he was out, the drunker he would be, and the angrier he would get. This was my life.

I tried to stay awake so I'd be ready to face him, but despite my dread, I fell into a fitful sleep. I woke up gasping for air. There was a heaviness about my chest I'd never felt before. I couldn't breathe and I broke into a cold sweat all over. My first thought was of Pa, figuring he had finally decided to snuff the life out of me, but as I squinted through the horror and pain, I could see he wasn't there. There wasn't nobody there.

I choked and gagged until it hurt, but try as I might, I couldn't breathe. I thought if I could reach out and touch the table beside my bed it would break the spell, but I couldn't move. I tried to kick out with my legs but they wouldn't budge. It was as if a blacksmith had placed his huge anvil on my chest and wrapped chains around my arms and legs. My heart was beating so hard I imagined I was not long for this world, and then I had a crazy thought: I imagined someone sitting on me, clutching me tight.

Then I felt the strange sensation of a thought enter my head as if someone had just told me a secret. It was an oddly comforting sensation in spite of my terror. In that instant, the chains binding me fell away and I intoned this thought out loud:

"Get away. Got to get away now."

I blinked through the sting in my sweat soaked eyes and took in a breath so deep it seemed like someone was pushing more air into my lungs than I could normally take in. I savored it; breathing suddenly felt like such a gift. I listened intently but everything was quiet. Pa still wasn't home, but I knew this only meant his wrath would soon be falling upon me.

I immediately decided I *had* to follow the notion that had entered my head.

"Get away now."

It seemed so real and it mirrored a fear I had long harbored. I assumed one of these days Pa would be sending me to join Mother. Not on purpose, mind you, but in the midst of his drunken rage, it seemed a very possible outcome. Perhaps, I thought, this was the day.

I lit a candle and changed out of my nightshirt. In the candlelight I noticed a faint, slightly raised mark forming on my shoulder, a bit like the outline of a crude sort of W. I put my shirt on over it and paid it no mind. I packed what meager belongings I had and made my way to the docks. It was the new moon and the streets were very dark. I pretty much knew where Pa hung out when drinking, so I avoided any of his likely paths, figuring that at this late hour, he would be too drunk to consider where I might have gone.

I remembered it was Thursday, and Captain Thompson regularly sailed the *Margaret Anne* up to Houston on that day every week. He had a slave, Johnson, who was slightly older than me, but he had been a friend from the docks for several years. Johnson and I had ridden the same boat a number of times in the past. The captain was a nice man who had decided to purchase Johnson as a means of protecting him from the usual uncertain life of servitude. Of course I knew it was a working boat and it gave the captain another hand to help load or unload cargo, but Johnson later told me it was the best thing that had ever happened to him, since he could still see his mama on occasion. He ate well, and the trips up the bayou were full of adventure.

Johnson was sleeping inside the coils of a rope in the stern of the boat when I arrived. All was quiet except for the slapping of the water against the sides of the ship and the slight moaning of the vessel itself. I crept aboard and shook his shoulder. He cracked one eye open and recognized me.

"Jack, what ya doing here...? Taking a trip wit us?"

I whispered, "I'm finally leaving home, Johnson...ever since my mama died, my pa has been on the brink of beating me to death because of it. I figure maybe to ride to Houston like I've always done but just get off there to hide from him. Can you help me hide my bundle from the captain?"

"Sho 'nuff, Jack."

He secreted the bundle behind some of the cargo and pointed to a spot nearby where I could remain somewhat hidden and I settled in. I promptly fell asleep.

In the morning, I awoke to the sounds of the ship being readied. I came out from my place of concealment, and Captain Thompson greeted me.

"Why, it's young Mr. Jack. Are you joining us today?"

I nodded meekly and he welcomed me into the small wheel house like he always did. Within a few minutes, we cast off. Captain Thompson was an expert in the ways of Buffalo Bayou, and on this day, the water was up so our passage was without incident. Several hours after leaving Galveston, we tied up at Allen's Landing in the heart of Houston.

There was always a hubbub of activity at the dock, so Captain Thompson's attention was diverted from me. "Captain, I'm going to go see Johnson."

He briefly acknowledged my statement and then paid me no heed.

Johnson was busy unloading cargo but looked up from his work and told me, "Jack, yer bundle is hiding over yonder behind those crates."

"Thanks, Johnson," I said, "will you cover for me?"

"Ah'll do mah best, Jack."

"Just tell them that as far as you know, I made the trip back with you."

Then his eyes widened and he stared at my chest. I looked down and noticed my shirt had shifted, revealing the mark I had noticed earlier.

"I knows that mark. You been ridden. *She* tell you to go?"

"I don't know what you mean."

"The *hag*. Well, it's best you skedaddle now, hear? Take care, Jack. I'll tell them what you said."

I looked back and couldn't see the captain anywhere, so I grabbed my bundle and quickly made my way off the boat. I slipped up an alley and meandered my way into the streets of Houston.

Three

I would not recommend my method of escape to anyone. I left without any plan and only a few coins. I paused several blocks away from the docks to catch my breath and noticed my bundle was bigger than I remembered. It was nothing more than a blanket wrapped around a shirt and a Bible and tied shut with some thin rope. When I opened it and found a half loaf of bread stuck in the top, I realized Johnson must have put it there. I sat and broke off a chunk, and while I chewed, I contemplated my new home of Houston.

I originally thought my father would follow me up the bayou if he stopped drinking long enough to consider any reasonable course of action. Still, I considered the notion he might figure I jumped a ship for parts unknown as well. I considered it. We boys prowled the docks and knew the routines of these boats. But the prospect of such a departure was such an unknown, I feared it even more than I feared Pa's wrath.

Another thought occurred to me: he might not even care that I was gone. I never seemed to do anything to his liking. After Mother died, his rage toward me increased. I guess I didn't exactly blame him because I made so many mistakes. But deep down I knew it was the drink, and I did blame him for drinking. Nobody should be made to endure a beating for no good reason.

I remembered how the old woman had stood up for me, risking the wrath of her master and of my father. Both men had backed down when faced with her fiery words and the cold stare of her milky eye. I still loved him, but I couldn't stand for the drinking.

I noticed a tree across the path from my resting place, and something carved into it caught my eye. When I approached it to investigate, I stopped in mid path.

"Ho, boy, get out of the road!"

I jumped forward to avoid being trampled by a horse and rider. I could see the markings now. VV. I looked around, but no one was paying any attention to it or to me.

There were many ways a boy could make himself useful in 1859 Houston. In some respects the town seemed busier than Galveston. It was growing, and there were new buildings being erected and a lot of horses, carriages, and wagons. All manner of stores and other business seemed to be prospering. Oftentimes a well-dressed gentleman would ride up on a horse and dismount to enter a business, and if he spied a youth standing there, would offer him a coin to watch his horse for a few minutes. That first day, I made enough money to buy me something more to eat. It was easy money made by just by standing around, but I knew I could not make a living by it.

For a few days, I slept where I could find a dry spot and enquired about some place where I might work for a roof over my head. I found a small livery stable where I swept and cleared out stalls and made a few coins. I kept low to the ground for fear the law would come looking for me, my father tagging along behind them, ready to drag me back to my life of torment. One day, a slightly built black man happened upon me.

"Hey, boy, you looking for a place to stay?"

"Who are you?"

"Name's Sylvester," he said. "Well, is you?"

"Yes," I said. "I'm an orphan, living day to day. I sure could use something."

"Old man name of Moze sent me looking for you. He heared you was creeping around. Sez he knows something 'bout you."

"I don't know no Moze but am willing to find out."

"Widow lady named Jenkins is the one you want to see. Old Moze is hers, if'n you can call it that. She be needing somebody to help her manage him."

"I ain't never heard of managing a slave." Then I remembered a word I had heard. "Overseer?"

"Naw, ain't like that at all," he said. "She gots the big white house two blocks this away," he pointed. "Go see her and find out about it." He waved and went on his way.

I walked two blocks in the direction Sylvester had pointed and sure enough found a big white house. A tree on the corner bore a faint impression of the same sign I had seen my first day. VV.

I opened the gate and, leaving my bundle at the bottom of the steps, I approached the door and knocked. A gray haired woman with a smiling face appeared.

"Yes, may I help you?"

I pulled off my cap. "Howdy, ma'am. I heard you might need some help here."

"I might, but who are you?"

"John Benson, ma'am, but folks mostly call me Jack. I'm... I'm an orphan."

"Dear boy, how old are you?"

"Thirteen, ma'am. My mama died of the consumption a few months ago. My daddy's long gone."

"My lord." She placed a hand to her chest. "You come on in, dear, and let me fix you something to eat."

I sat at a table as familiar smells filled the house and soon I had a heap of bacon, scrambled eggs, and biscuits filling my stomach to the point of popping.

"There, dear, you must feel better."

"Yes, ma'am... I ain't...I mean, I don't think I've eaten like that in a long time."

"So you don't have a single aunt, uncle, or cousin who might take you in?"

"No, ma'am."

"Now I can't pay you, understand, but I do need someone I can trust."

"You can trust me, ma'am."

"You can call me Mrs. Jenkins—I'm a widow."

"Yes, Mrs. Jenkins, you can trust me. Just tell me what I need to do."

"I've got...well, my servant...I've owned him for about forty years. He came with us all the way from Georgia, I lease him out as a tracker and a hunter. He is the best there is. He also keeps meat on our table."

"A hunter?"

"Yes, but...well, of course, being a slave, he can't very well just carry a gun, can he?"

"No, ma'am."

"I need someone who can accompany him, carry the gun and powder and such. I think a thirteen year old will do. I must warn you, though, he is old and set in his ways. He's a cantankerous old fool, but I can't bear to sell him. He's run off the last three handlers I've hired. Well, to be truthful, he found them stealing from me." She raised her eyebrows and scrutinized me with a deep thoughtful gaze. Then her face softened. "Do you think you could do this kind of work for me?"

"Yes, ma'am."

"Like I said, I couldn't pay you money, well, perhaps a little, but for the most part, you will get food and a roof over your head. Moze stays in a room out in the barn. You'd live in a room next to him."

"Sound's fine, Mrs. Jenkins."

She took me by the hand, led me to the back door, and called out, "Moze!"

A large black man emerged from a side door of the small barn.

"Yes'm?"

"Moze, this is Jack...he's our new man."

"Man? Looks like a boy t'me."

"Never you mind, you old fool. Now you go on now and show him his room."

Moze laughed, showing a full set of teeth, "Yes'm. C'mon now, young'un."

Four

I followed Moze into what they called a barn, but it was more what I would call a shed. Well, it did have stalls for a horse and a cow. Across from those stalls were two small rooms, each big enough for a straw mattress. Right outside the rooms there was a worn table and two chairs.

"Sit down here and let's talk," Moze said, pointing to one of the chairs.

He sat heavily on the other chair with a slight groan and I sat next to him. He looked me up and down and almost sneered.

"I know who you are...yer daddy lives yonder in Galveston. I hears he is looking for you, mostly drunk as a skunk. Do he beat on you, Jack?"

"It got worse after my ma died. Like he blamed me for her being dead."

"I'm sho he do. That come with the territory. I means with the booze. Your first lesson here with me is there will be no such foolishness here at Miz Jenkins. You hear me?"

"I– I– I've lived with the bad side of whiskey my whole life. I don't even like to walk by a saloon."

"You listen to me, boy, you stay away from it forever and your life will be the better for it. It is the elixir of the devil," he said, wagging a finger in my direction. "I've been drunk exactly one time, and it made me sick as a dog, and you know what?"

I shook my head.

"I deserved it. That proved to me that it is poison. You drinks poison you either gets sick or you die." Moze had stood as he began this discourse but now he settled his large frame down in the other chair and sighed. "Ah's gettin to be too old to train me another one o' you idjits."

"What do you mean?"

"What she say your job is here with me?"

"I didn't rightly understand... something about accompanying you on hunting trips."

"Something like that. Listen up, chile, this here society calls me a slave. I reckon I am but here, in this here barn, I'm the boss. You understand?"

I merely nodded, transfixed by his discourse. Moze was intent on manifesting his presence and impressing upon me his place in our small world.

"That's the long and the short of it. This here is my world. The widow Jenkins been as good to me as any an angel can be on this earth, but the truth of the matter is, I ain't no hired hand. I reckon the good Lawd puts us here to fulfill our purpose, and for whatever His reasons are, right now this here is mine. Listen, boy, I've seen a lot of this country and I've done me two handfuls of different jobs in my life, but what I'ze best at is tracking and hunting. Sure I do my chores around here. You ever see a cleaner barn?"

I looked around and uttered a meek, "No."

"'Course not! I'll teach you the ways and the means of that, too. Like I said, this here's MY world. Now this accompaniment she talked about. The white man's world, your world, says a black man, a slave that is, can't be carrying no gun. Sech foolishness. I'ze the best tracker and hunter in the state, and the best shot! Ever-body knows that. Ain't none better. Miz Jenkins found out a long time ago that she could hire me out like some stud bull or something. Once we gets out in the woods and I gets wind of a big fat buck or maybe a wolf that's been terrorizin' folks, ain't nobody sez nothing 'bout givin me no gun. I'm old but I still got me my eyes and I lay a bead on 'em and drop 'em. You just there to hand me my gun. You got that?"

"I guess."

"You *guess*?"

"I mean, yes, I understand. How old are you, Moze?"

"Sech a fool question but about typical for a young'un. How old is YOU?"

"Thirteen."

"You're jes a chile. Lawdy sakes alive. I am somewhere's around seventy years of age. Don't rightly know. Ain't nobody much keeping track of the birthdays of no slaves, now is there?

"I don't rightly know."

"Well, take it from me, they don't." He pointed to the room on the right. "That's where you sleep. You keep it clean."

"I will."

"Ah surely don't want to scare you none, Jack, but we just have to get these things established."

"Moze...I understand. I'm happy to have a roof over my head and some food to eat."

"You gots that here. This here can be a good life for slave or boy. Ah jes don't want no foolishness here between us. You'll see... out on a job I can play the fool just like any other fool slave. Slavery ain't nothing but a dead serious game. We po black folks ain't got the cards the white folks do, but if'n we play what cards we got right, we do okay. I'ze had a lot worse massahs than the widow, that's for sure. I'ze seen a lot in my years, most of it bad."

Moze leaned forward and looked me in the eye. "Open the top of your shirt." He pointed toward my shoulder, "Right there."

I pulled my shirt open, revealing the mark.

"I thoughts so," he said, "I rightly felt it."

"Felt what?"

"How you think I knowed enough about you to send Sylvester to fetch you here? Vanita Valine. That's her mark. She been hag riding you." He pulled his shirt open and showed me the same mark, less noticeable against his dark skin but there just the same. "Me and her go way back. Mostly as friends because I know better than to cross her."

He stood again. He didn't look quite as big. I could see that although his frame had once been more powerful, skin sagged against bones and his face was gaunt. He was wearing a cap and gray hair poked out around it. He was maybe as tall as Pa, perhaps just a shade taller. He walked over to the horse's stall.

"Git over here, boy. This here is Elvira. She's good as a draft horse or a riding horse. You know anything about horses?"

I shook my head. "My father has a horse but I never did much for it except feed it."

Moze proceeded to take on the role of teacher and began to show me how to take care of Elvira. This was the core of our life together. In the barn we were teacher and student. He talked tough, in an almost intimidating low tone, but it made me listen even more carefully and learn. Over the coming days, we became even more than teacher and student...we became friends.

It was not very long before we went out on our first hunting trip together. Two rich men from New Orleans had come to Houston on business and had paid the widow Jenkins for Moze's services. I rode Elvira and Moze sat behind me. Sometimes he walked alongside. I had the gun, an old flintlock strapped to a harness attached to the saddle. Moze directed us to a spot in a large stand of woods about an hour or so north of town.

"This here's da spot, gentlemen."

We all dismounted, and I carried the weapon carefully, as I had been instructed. Moze tied the horses to nearby saplings. The men were what Pa would have called dandies, dressed too nicely to be tromping out in the woods. They had bottles of whiskey in their saddlebags and were drinking and smoking cigars. They both had fine sporting pieces.

We all walked behind Moze until he motioned for us to stop. He pointed, and I could see a fine buck in the distance. He reached back, and I handed him our gun, which he quietly loaded and handed back to me, never taking his eyes off the deer. The men loaded their guns as well, taking about twice the time Moze had taken. The buck was about a hundred yards away. The men raised their guns and both fired in unison. They were not good shots. The deer bounded away.

"Don't matter, he won't go far," Moze said and we continued on foot.

He held up his hand. We stopped.

"What did I tell you," he said. "There he is. He's thinking maybe it was a spot of thunder."

"You take him, Moze. We hear you are the best shot around," one of the men whispered.

Moze looked back at me and smiled. "Ah surely don't know about that, but I'll try."

I handed him the gun, and he expertly raised the piece, took aim and fired. In the flash and smoke of the shot, the buck went down. The men had their prize. In short order, Moze field dressed the buck, a fine eight pointer, and strapped it down to one of the mounts.

"Who would have thought a nigger could be such a shot."

Moze continued working through this dialogue, but I could tell something about the statement pained him.

Back in the barn, when I took the saddle off Elvira and brushed her out, I asked Moze about his reaction.

"Listen here, chile, nothing cuts through a black man's soul more than that word."

"I've heard slaves use it...everybody uses it."

"Don't make it right. It feels just the same. It ain't a word I use." He grabbed a pail and started feeding Elvira. "Listen, people gets what's called habits. Some habits is good, like going to church and sech, and some habits is bad. That's one of the bad ones."

"I'm not sure I understand. It's just a word."

"Some words is harmless. Some words, like that one, is from the devil. I gots no use for anybody using it, black or white, slave or free man. Let me tell you something. Did you hear them tell ME I was a good shot?"

"He told you he had heard you were a good shot."

"That was before, when he wanted me to do something for him, something he couldn't do himself, even with his fine clothes and expensive gun. After the deer was down, he was talking like I wasn't even there. Like I was the blamed horse."

I thought for a second, remembering the conversation and realized Moze was exactly right.

He set the bucket down. "What you think about all this slave business?"

"I don't rightly know. It's the way it is. I played with all kinds of kids most of my life."

"Darker kids was most likely slaves."

"I kind of knew that, but to me they was just friends."

"And where them friends now?"

"One, Johnson, works on the steamer that brought me here."

"Works? Or is a slave on that there boat?"

"Slave."

"So he gots no say in the matter, do he?"

"I guess not."

"No. I know the boy you're talking about, not much older than you. He's like me. Got hisself a good situation. Most ain't got that. Most gots beatings and sometimes worse. We are *people*, Jack. Jes like you. Slaves gets married and has chillun just like white folks. 'Cepting they can get sold out from under one another."

"Really?"

"Happened to me. I had me a young wife back in Georgia. Hain't seen or hear'd nothing about her since Mister Jenkins done bought me and brought me here."

"That's awful, Moze. Did you have children?"

"Yes, just mo slaves. Ain't gots no idea 'bout them either. It ain't fair, but you got one thing right. It's just the way it is. I hear tell some folks up north working to change things. It's a mighty powerful thing they trying to change. Won't never come easy."

"Abolitionists?" I almost whispered the word because the merest mention of it would spur a drunken outrage from Pa and would unleash a wave of anguish, hatred, and despair from others.

"Yes, sir. Surely the notion is growing. I hear tell they's folks helping to spirit runaways on up to the North and freedom."

"You ever going to run away, Moze?"

He laughed. "I'm too old to go gallivanting off to something I don't know nothing about. I gots me a good situation here. In my own way I gots respect. And what's an old man like me going to do with freedom? I'm like you; I'm happy enough to have what I gots...food and a dry place to sleep."

I thought often about this conversation with Old Moze. In my experience, even though I'd only had thirteen years to dwell on it, black folks was just that, folks. And abolitionists? It was a concept far beyond my comprehension. Politics was something I heard in snatches of conversation on the street. But newspapers talked a lot over the next year about John Brown and a man named Lincoln. Even a boy like me could feel the winds of change were blowing. I didn't know then, but they were blowing up into a fierce storm.

Five

Sure, Old Moze showed me how to track, hunt, and fish, but he taught me how to take care of chickens, horses, and cows, too. In fact, Old Moze taught me more about life than anyone else. He had a deep understanding of right and wrong, and he never missed an opportunity to clarify lessons from everyday experiences. With my mother gone and Pa drunk all the time, it was the learning I reckon I had missed in those in-between years. It seemed like we'd known each other for a lifetime, but in all, it was only about two years.

I didn't much understand the workings of politics at fourteen, but there was an increasing hoopla in the years 1860 and 1861. Talk on Market Square, a sort of central gathering place in Houston for commerce and information, seemed to center on the candidacy of Mr. Lincoln to the presidency. People were quite worked up about the prospect of an abolitionist as president.

"We are doomed as a country."

"This will destroy our way of life."

If someone tried to take a moderate view, "Let's see what he does," they would be jeered at and pushed into the shadows of some alleyway where rough sounds would be heard.

As near as I could tell, the only thing this Mr. Lincoln proposed to do was stop slavery from expanding into new states. The more I'd grown to know about slavery, the less I agreed with the notion. I knew I couldn't change it myself, but I didn't see this as a bad thing. I was just one person and a boy at that.

Then one day, something big had happened, and the talk on the streets was all about it. South Carolina had seceded. I was confused when I first heard that word, but Moze explained it to me.

"They's cut themselves off from the whole country. They fools if they thinks they can make it alone. I've lived there, and there ain't enough of nothing there for them to make it without the rest. It's like your little finger cuttin' itself off and thinkin' it can do the work of the whole hand. It don't work. It's just going to shrivel up to nothing."

But that was just the beginning. The news filtered down...one state after another was pulling out and joining together into a new country, and the word on the street was that people wanted Texas to do the same. Our governor, Mr. Sam Houston, was dead set against it.

I was confused about the issues, but then again, I was little more than a boy. At the age of fourteen, I was big enough to think I knew more about the world than I really did. Of course, things were much more complicated than I supposed.

Every chance I got, I would read Moze newspaper stories by candlelight. In January of 1861, secession fever ran high, and there was much whooping and hollering when the secession convention voted to secede from the United States.

"They've done it, Moze."

Moze stared into the shadows of the clapboard siding. "Nothing but grief will come of it."

A short time later there was more whooping and hollering when Texas joined the Confederate states. In the midst of this, Sam Houston was stopped from being governor. According to what I read, he was fine and good for Texas to go it alone, as they had done in the years after the San Jacinto battle, but he thought joining up with a new country was a mistake.

Still, for Moze and me, well, we had our chores to keep us busy, so all of these things swirled around us like a whirlwind. Mrs. Jenkins would oftentimes send me on errands that took me past Market Square. I began to see the recruitment stations that had become a regular part of life down there. People reckoned there was going to be a fight, so various regiments were being formed to help protect Texas and the Confederacy. As each of these militia units formed, they'd establish camps on the outside of the city. Most of them moved on after they finished recruiting.

On my errands I would sometimes hang around and listen to the speeches. These usually started off by talking bad things about the people of the north and Mr. Lincoln. Then they'd start in singing the praises of the state's rights, and some almost wanted to grant sainthood to Jefferson Davis. There was a lot of flowery sentiment, but it all seemed like a lot of words to me, so I would go on about my business.

Still the impressive officers' uniforms were an inspiring sight and many boys like me conspired about ways to lie and convince recruiters to accept them. There was such a hurry to build up an army, it seemed to me that many of the officers were not too picky. If you were big for your age and you could get someone to vouch for you, you might could manage to sign yourself in. I knowed a number of boys who did that very thing.

One day, the news from South Carolina sounded bad. Cannons had been fired when a fort called Sumter in Charleston harbor refused to surrender. After reading this story to Moze, I saw a tear fall down the side of his face.

"That there's the straw that's gonna break the camel's back. It's gonna mean war."

It didn't seem like it to me. With so much military activity in Texas, I could only imagine how much there was in other states of the Confederacy. How could the Union hope to fight a war with us? It was all anyone on the street could talk about. I admit that I was so caught up in the romance and pageantry of everything, it almost seemed like a good thing, despite what Moze had said. It's like when the fair comes to town. You never give such things a thought until they come down the streets, parading and blowing horns, and setting up for their shows. But you get caught up in the event, and the only thing you can think of doing is to go over there and see it.

Moze didn't see it the same way at all. One day after reading to him about the first big battle, up in Virginia at Manassas, he did his best to set me straight.

"This here is the worst thing in the world, and there's going to be the devil to pay. You'll see. Ain't nothing different 'bout this here Confederate nation they calls it, 'cepting to keep folks like me as property. You knows how ah feels about dat. Sure, they talks about taxes and things, but it all boils down to keeping their slaves. They thought that Lincoln fella was going to free us or something, but I never heared any solid words from him to that end."

I countered, "I know, but I think there's more to it." I had stars in my eyes from hearing all the speeches and seeing all the splendid uniforms.

"Oh, I knows all 'bout them flashy clothes, shiny muskets, and swords dangling. It's all a young boy like you sees. And that's okay. It's what they's expecting you to see. Remember, in the old days my peoples was warriors from far off in Africa. It's in my blood. You young'uns think it's all glory doing battle. Sure, there's some o' that, but nobody knows better than me what them muskets can do to hide and bone. There's gonna be a lot of death and a lot of grief. Glory comes at a price. And for what?"

Our conversations would follow this tone every time we talked about it. Come October, as my fifteenth birthday approached, I tarried more and more around the recruiters on the square. I had grown quite a bit taller and I was as big as most men. Regular hard work had seasoned my features as well. Around this time, Moze started calling me "Captain" Jack as a new nickname. I think he was making fun of my military aspirations, but the name stuck and most everybody in our circle, excepting the widow Jenkins, copied Moze's example.

More and more I made mention to the notion of joining up. "I'm really thinking of doing it, Moze."

"Don't be in such a rush, Captain Jack."

But this thought of me leaving to join in the fight seemed to draw the weight of all Moze's years down hard on his shoulders. He was slowing down, and I see now how my talk of joining up was having an ill effect on him. In November, he got a bad cold and it settled hard in his chest. He couldn't seem to shake it. I'd stay up nights listening to him wheeze and cough. Mrs. Jenkins had to depend on me to keep meat on the table. Luckily I had learned Moze's lessons well.

I tended to him as best as I could, but he kept pushing me away. "Just leave me be, Captain Jack."

Close to Christmas I had another fitful night's sleep. Moze had suffered through a fearful amount of hacking and coughing all day, and I was worried about him. My room was cold with the chill from a blue 'norther that had blown in earlier in the day and I shivered while I dozed under my blanket. Suddenly I was thrust flat on my back with my eyes wide open. I couldn't breathe. Beads of freezing cold sweat formed all over my body as I struggled in vain to move, but none of my muscles could so much as twitch. I gagged against a force on the center of my chest that was preventing any breath at all. I tried to call out to Moze, but I could make no sound. A wave of fear swept over me, and I was afraid consumption was inflicting itself on me just as it did my mother. Then the notion of a thought entered my brain as if someone had just whispered a secret in my ear.

"Moze needs you."

All at once, the weight on my chest vanished and, with what seemed like a gentle push, I could fill my lungs again. I coughed against the chilly air, thrust myself to my feet, and hurried to Moze's room.

Through labored panting he asked me, "Captain Jack, is that you?"

"Yes, I'm here."

"You know the old trick-doctor Vanita?"

"Yes. She scares me, Moze."

"She scares everybody, that's what she does. But I needs to see her. Fetch her over here. Please?"

I hadn't seen Vanita since the day on the boat, but I remembered the mark Moze said she had left on both of our shoulders. Mine had faded with time, but as I got dressed in the dim candlelight, I could see the outlines of the two V's had returned.

I saddled and mounted Elvira and set out in the middle of the chilly night. Pickell's homestead was on the other side of the town. On the way, I thought about my time with Vanita on the boat a couple of years earlier. She was a small wiry woman with a disposition different from any other slave I had ever met. On the dark boat ride, she was sweet and consoling to me, but once Pa lifted his fist to hit me, she raised up and acted like a riled up bobcat. In that moment, everybody was afraid of her, even her master.

I could see her up ahead, waiting on the path just outside the main house as I approached. She was bundled up and looked older than I remembered. I imagined she was too old to work the fields, but I assumed she could still do some chores around the place, like tending to his chickens. When one delved into owning slaves, they were yours to care for even when they got old. But in her case, I supposed there was likely an element of concern, for she was widely known and feared as a trick doctor, a practitioner of hoodoo. Most God-fearing people dismissed hoodoo as harmless superstition, but as usual, Moze had set me straight on the subject.

"They is ancient things nobody can explain. These involve beliefs that are far different from the teachings of the Bible. It ain't counter to the Bible, mind you, it sort of takes a roundabout shortcut alongside what most folks considers good. But it ain't bad, at least not especially. The hoodoo *can* be used for bad, but it can be used the other way, too."

From what I had heard, a lot of it had to do with herbs and tinctures a practitioner like Vanita knew how to concoct. People might call on a trick doctor if they needed some ailment tended to. Like as not, this was what I assume Moze wanted her for. But I also knew others would seek her out for some of her darker work. Some folks aspired to have spells cast for love, but just as often, there were spells for harm or revenge.

I was scared of that aspect of her. When I saw her waiting, I thought back to the night Pa had told me she was a hag rider. I suddenly realized she had used some of those powers to rouse me to inquire about Moze's deteriorating state the same way she had earlier warned me to leave Pa.

I took a deep breath and pulled Elvira to a slow walk. Moze wanted to see her, and I endeavored to fulfill his wish. Vanita stared at me as I approached. Her facial features and lighter complexion differed from many slaves, and this served to enhance her terrifying presence. Moze had told me her grandfather was a Seminole Indian and her father was some white man she never knew.

"Wut choo want, Captain Jack?"

"It's Moze."

"Ah expect he wants to see me. Ah been waiting."

"You knew I was coming?"

"Hush, chile. What you think I standing out here in the cold for?" She looked up at me. Her one cloudy eye always drew my attention first, but the other eye blazed black with a fire unlike anything I had seen. I instinctively pulled back on the reins, causing Elvira to make a slight noise.

"Ah've told you before, you don't need to be afeared when I'm with you." She picked up the large bag at her feet. "Let's go tend to my business."

The front door of the house opened as I reached to grab her bag, and we were confronted by farmer Pickell. He had obviously been awakened by the sound of my horse.

"Where you going with my woman, boy?"

She spoke up before I had a chance to answer. "Death is knocking on old Moze the hunter's door, mistah. Ah needs to go tend to him."

This was apparently not an uncommon occurrence, yet the farmer seemed to avert his eyes from her gaze.

"All right but, boy, you have her back here as soon as you can."

I nodded and hoisted the old woman, who was surprisingly spry, up behind me on the horse.

She again answered for herself. "I reckon I'll be back when my work is done and not before."

We rode through the cold together, and back at the widow Jenkins' place, I led her into Moze's room.

"Boil me some water, Captain Jack."

We had a small firebox for some heat and it served as a small stove, so I stoked the fire and set a pot to boil on top of it. I could hear them whispering but was not close enough to hear what they were saying. Vanita emerged from the room with Moze's tin cup and handed it to me. There was a handful of herbs and bark in it.

"Go ahead and pour yer water in here."

I complied, and a woodsy aroma filled the room.

"I have to tell you something, Captain Jack. He's not long for this world. This will help settle him, make him more comfortable. But there ain't nothing ah's can do to save him."

She left a bundle on the table.

"Gives him a cup or two of these roots and herbs every so often."

"I will."

She took the cup into Moze's room and in a few more minutes came back out and said she was ready to leave.

She didn't say a word as we rode along, but when we got close to her master's place, she tapped me on the shoulder and said, "Stops right here."

When she got off the horse she asked me to join her, so I dismounted.

"Ah needs to tell you something."

"What is it?" I asked.

"Old Moze didn't want me for my tincture of herbs, he wanted to tell me something 'bout you, Captain Jack."

"What?"

"He wants me to protect you. Paid me good money, too."

"Paid you?"

"You know slaves got some monies squirreled away for a rainy day."

"I know that."

"He paid me and I will do it. He say he knows you's going to join up with one of the soldier groups forming. Dang fool thing for a youngster like you. War is the worstest thing they is."

I looked down at the ground.

"I done already cast the first spell. Ain't nothing you can do about it, but you'll see the workings of it no matter where you go."

She tapped the area of my shoulder where she'd left her mark. "You understand, right?"

I sheepishly rubbed at the spot, "I do."

She then handed me a small bundle in a red flannel bag.

"This here is your trick bag—it's part of the protection. Always keep it close and don't bother looking in it. There ain't nothing in there. It's for protection and to remind you I'm with you. Stick it in the light of a full of the moon when you can. This will help you appreciate its potential. Understand?"

"Yes." I stuffed the bag into my pocket.

"Captain Jack, I needs to tell you something else. Listen up now, this is important."

"I'm listening." I fixed my gaze on the cloudy eye; it seemed to be looking right through me and into my soul.

"This a fool's errand you running on. Them Confederates don't knows it yet, but they's not gonna save slavery...they's gonna be fighting to end it. I sees it clear as day." She chuckled slightly before continuing. "Slavery's got too big a hold on them people, and they ain't never gonna let it go without a fight. You know, the country coulda growed up and cast off these chains in maybe fifty or a hunnert years, but mark my words, four or five years of fighting is going to seal the deal and end this thing cold. Trust me, they ain't gonna win this war. I sees it. That's why I agreed to protect you."

She chuckled. "You's gonna be fighting to help free us all, you just don't knows it yet. But I'm bound to protect you as best as I can, so I'll do it. Take care, Captain Jack." Then she gave me a slight smile and touched my cheek with the scarred palm of her hand before sauntering down the path to the farm. I could hear her giggling to herself as she walked.

I touched the bag in my pocket, then remounted Elvira and rode back home.

Moze was just as we had left him. He didn't look good.

"Did she do it, Captain Jack?"

"Do what?"

"Tell you what I wanted of her."

I pulled out the trick bag.

"No, no, put that away, but now I know she done as I asked her. You keep it safe and do as she told you. It's the best I can do to protect you when I'ze gone."

Old Moze passed from this earth a few hours later, on Christmas Day, 1861. I buried him myself the next day in an old slave burying ground over by the Buffalo Bayou. My friend Johnson from the steamer *Margaret Anne* helped me.

"Should we say nothing?" he asked as we laid Moze in the ground.

I recited something from memory, "The Lord is my shepherd…"

After I finished the roughshod version of the Twenty-Third Psalm, Johnson said, "God bless you, Mr. Moze."

"Amen," I said with tears streaming down my face.

The very next day, I noticed a new recruiting effort underway over in Market Square with a flashy French sounding colonel named DeBray. His uniform was splendidly outfitted and he seemed the very essence of a real military man. A man told me he had been trained at some exclusive soldiering school in France. I curiously watched their efforts all the next day before I made my decision. That night I informed Mrs. Jenkins of my plans.

"Aren't you too young?"

"Perhaps, ma'am, but I'm going to try. It is my duty…at least I think it is."

"Remember, this is still your home as long as you need it to be. You've been a good companion to old Moze and have been every bit as good a handyman around here as he was. I know every young man in the county wants to go fight for our new country, so those of us who remain just have to go about our lives as best as we can." I could see tears welling up in her eyes.

"Yes, ma'am."

"What will you do in the Army, Jack?"

"There's been some right nice cavalry outfits recruiting over at Market Square."

"Oh, my, the cavalry? Why, you will need a horse, won't you?"

I hadn't even thought about it.

"Take Elvira... take her as my parting gift to you. You've been good to me, and you were very good with Moze. You deserve it. She's a good horse."

"Thank you, ma'am."

I started the next morning with a lie. I walked right up to a man who introduced himself as Captain Hare and signed my paper and let the doc poke and prod me and make his measurements. I spent the rest of the day hanging around on Market Square with a small group of other recruits. Toward noon, we all spoke the oath of allegiance to the Confederate States of America, and we began our new adventure in DeBray's Brigade of Texas Cavalry, soon to be known as the 26th Texas Cavalry of the Confederate States. It was the turning point of my young life. It was December 28, 1861, and I was fifteen years old.

Six

There were several recruits that day. Captain Hare told me I'd be serving under him in Company K of DeBray's Brigade. He never asked my age. The biggest question when signing up was whether I had a horse. I pointed out Elvira. I had brushed and spruced her that morning, just the way Moze had showed me, and her coat shimmered like an evening star. Captain Hare looked her up and down, checked her hooves and teeth, and decided she might be a little rough for cavalry work but she would do for now.

"You better save your money, Jack, she may not last the war," he joked.

The recruits were made to hang around Market Square while new prospects were encouraged to sign. There were only a few inquiries because the December weather was blustery and not too many individuals were out and about. The captain was accompanied by a sergeant who stood at attention most of the time while the captain talked about enlistment. We recruits were all young, full of vim and vigor, and we sometimes got loud in a bit of braggadocio.

"I'm going to kill me a dozen Yanks."

"I'll get me a hunnert!"

"I'll lay a swath of them all the way to Washington City!"

When we got too loud in our joking, the sergeant would come over and talk to us.

"Yer soldiers now. Quiet up and act like it."

My coat was threadbare and I started to take a chill. I think the other fellas were feeling the cold also, so the sergeant gathered some wood for us from a nearby wagon and we set to work making a small fire. The chill helped quiet us down as we huddled together warming ourselves.

Shortly after noon, the sergeant told us to gather our belongings and our horses. Once we were mounted, he led us to the brigade's encampment on the western outskirts of town. After we had ridden a while, I saw it—rows of tents and some makeshift corrals. I recognized the area, since Moze and I had hunted there several times. I knew the nearby thickets might keep rabbit stew on our menu for months at a time.

"I'm the master sergeant, I serve between you and the officers. If you have any concerns, you come to me."

I knew little about army life, so I tried to pay close attention. Of course I already knew the basics. The officers were in charge, followed by the sergeants, and soon we would have corporals appointed or elected. Company K was one of the last companies in the brigade, and Captain Hare was intent on recruiting a hundred men to fill out our ranks. Colonel DeBray had managed to secure supplies from US army stores our militia had seized after the secession when local militia troops had assumed control over a military depot in San Antonio. That is where most of the tents had come from.

After we dismounted at the camp, he marched us in rough order over to the supply sergeant where we were shown an array of captured equipment. Although cavalry usually wore boots, there were no boots, only brogan style shoes for us common soldiers. We were given three options: picking from these shoes, buying boots in town, or wearing the shoes we had. My shoes were worn, so I chose a pair of the military shoes that fit me fairly well. The short jackets were all confederate gray and the trousers were union blue. This was all they had.

"The state of Texas has provided these jackets for the new brigade," the supply sergeant had said, "but the trousers and shoes all came from the depot in San Antonio. You lot are lucky ones since there is a bit of a choice."

As we made sure we had outfits we could fit into, there was a lot of joking and jostling. The shirts were either blue cotton or undyed white cotton. I could only find a white one that fit. I didn't mind too much, except it didn't look quite as military as the others. The short wool uniform jackets were scratchy and new, but they were warmer and did help cut the chill of the December afternoon. I tucked my trick bag into my trousers when I changed.

We were marched to a row of tents not far from our horses and instructed to set our belongings in tents. Some tents were already occupied by other recruits and some were empty. These shelters slept two or three. Another recruit and I chose an empty one, and inside we found stacks of blankets and some tin cups and plates we assumed we'd be using for meals. We each took a blanket and a set of the tin-ware and laid claim to a side of the tent.

A different sergeant appeared and stood just outside the row of tents with his hands on his hips. He had a permanent scowl etched across his face. He commenced to scream in a voice that seemed permanently hoarse.

"Get out here on the quick and stand in line so I can get a better look at you! Fall in!"

We dropped what we were doing, rushed out of the tent and stood in a line in front of our tents. He took a good long look at us and shook his head.

"To think this would happen to me in this lifetime. Lord take me now. You are the scruffiest lot of so-called soldiers I've ever laid eyes on," he said with a distinct Irish brogue. "I know I'll be crying myself to sleep tonight."

He walked along the line, taking great care to adjust our feet with a nudge and a gentle kick till we had them placed the way he wanted. He stopped at each one of us to do this. Then he adjusted the placement of our heads, taking care to tell us to look straight ahead and not to move unless he moved us. He adjusted our shoulders and finally, our hands.

"THAT, me fine feathered friends, is how a military man stands to attention. You'll find Colonel DeBray demands discipline in his brigade. You may see other units of this glorious army, especially from this god-forsaken wasteland of a state, who lack the discipline one learns in a real army, but your commander craves it. He was trained at a very fine academy from France, learning from the traditions instilled by Napoleon himself. So when I scream ATTENTION, this here is what you do. Every time. On the quick."

Then he let loose a chuckle and many of us relaxed our stance.

"ATTENTION!" and we all snapped into our previous pose.

He grinned. "Aye, you're pretty gawd-awful, but you'll get better with time. You have to, or I'll kick you on your sweet arse."

He pointed. "Down there is the mess tent. You grab your plates and cups and head down and draw rations. We're still a little informal today... most of the time you'll be handling your own provisions, but today we'll give you a little something extra to help coddle you boys through to another day. ATTENTION."

We snapped to attention again. "At ease." And we relaxed. He moved his arm in a sweeping gesture toward the mess tent, and we broke ranks, retrieved our plates and cups, and followed him down to the mess area. There were big pots boiling something that smelled faintly of beef. There may have been beef in it, but it was mostly chunks of onions, carrots, and potatoes. Off to one side there was a mush of cornmeal. We each got steaming portions of both items which burned our fingers as we tried to grasp the tin plates.

In the distance, we saw other recruits riding in with another sergeant at the lead. These were from other companies. We carried our plates back to our tents and ate inside to get out of the chill. I retrieved a spoon I had brought from my bag, but some of the others just shoveled the food into their mouths with their fingers when it had cooled enough. It wasn't much and it was far from good, but it was our first taste of Army food and it warmed our bellies. I know I was mighty hungry and figured the other fellows were as well.

After we had eaten, the sergeant returned and told us where to procure some hay for our horses along with other minor instructions regarding the layout of the camp. In accordance with Army discipline, we were told to remain in the vicinity of our company at all times unless instructed to go elsewhere. He told us that for the time being we would be taking care of our own horses, but as the company was filled out, there would be regular duties assigned. He gave us some general instructions in how to march, and we moved in rough unison to the hay wagon and then returned with armloads of hay to feed our horses. We were then shown where we could get some firewood and were again reminded that in the near future these duties would be assigned. Each of us grabbed an armful of firewood and marched back to our tent area.

Several new recruits were arriving for Company K when we returned, and after we built our fire, we observed the new recruits and smiled at each other as the sergeant lectured them in precisely the same way he had previously done with us. It was, I assumed, a practiced routine of indoctrinating fledgling soldiers in the ways of Army life.

It takes a lot of work for a military camp to operate, and even in this early stage of my career, the organization of it all amazed me. I had watched both my ma and the widow Jenkins manage a single home, and it seemed an endless task to me. But here in front of me I saw the same thing at a level designed for maybe a thousand souls. Even a brief glimpse revealed tents lined up in orderly rows, sections of the camp designed to hold troops, horses, supplies of food, firewood, water, and even fodder for the horses.

Moze and I had had our regular chores, and I knew there would be chores aplenty at this camp, some of them not too agreeable. A thousand men meant a thousand horses, perhaps more, because there were wagons to carry the supplies such an army would need. There were beef cattle to tend to as well.

"An army marches on its stomach," was one snatch of a conversation I heard on the streets of Houston as the country prepared itself to face this war. I thought it was funny when I heard it, but now it made sense to me. A thousand men meant a thousand meals several times a day, every day. And I was only looking at DeBray's brigade. There were many such brigades, not just in Texas, but in every state of the Confederacy. I assumed it was the same for the Union fellows as well. War was big business.

Growing up, I had only heard tell of stories of the war for Texas independence, the Mexican war, and the revolutionary war. I'd seen soldiers, mostly passing through on their way to serve various outposts in western Texas, but to me entire armies seemed more like unreal things one only read about in books. I imagined armies in battle to be like chess pieces moving on a board. Now I could see they were comprised of men, animals, and all manner of things to keep them alive and moving.

It all required constant organization and work. I felt my stomach growl as I pondered these things and expected it would growl many more times before it was all over. I assumed hunger would be a regular thing in the army, so I just ignored the pangs and resolved myself to get used to it for the duration. I'd signed up and there wasn't nothing much I could do about it now.

The mood was pensive as we warmed ourselves by the fire, and I assumed the other fellows were thinking the same thoughts as me. Toward the onset of dusk, we saw the tall presence of Captain Hare coming into camp, his recruiting over for the day. Behind him came another group of new cavalrymen. How raw and unpolished they looked to us veterans. I could see the smiles on the other men with me by the light of the fire...we were all thinking the same thing. Compared to the new men, we all imagined we were old hands at this army business now.

Seven

We warmed ourselves by the fire, chatting as we shivered in the December chill. The tent-mate fate had joined me with was crouching next to me.

"I'm John Benson, but everybody calls me Jack," I said.

"Robert. J. White."

"You from Houston? My folks lived in Galveston, but I've been living in Houston for the last two years," I said.

"Yep. Me and my ma live just outside the town. She's a widow woman but has a gentleman caller of late showing her a lot of attention, and I'm feeling a little put out so I decided it might be a good time for me to join up and see the world."

"How old are you?" I asked. He looked young, like me.

Robert looked around and whispered, "Sixteen. Don't tell no one. Supposed to be older, but Captain Hare didn't even ask me my age. He said as long as I was healthy and stout and had a good horse, he was fine with me."

I confessed in a similar low tone, "I– I'm fifteen. Hearing you are sixteen makes me feel a good bit better about my own tiny bit of convincing."

He patted me on the shoulder, "Tarnation, Jack, hearing about you makes me feel better, too. We can help each other out, don't you think?"

"Of course I do," I said. "You done much schooling?"

"My ma helped me with my letters and numbers and such. I did a little schooling, but after my pa died, I had to grab what work I could find to help out. Seems Ma will have someone else to help her now. How about you?"

"My ma did the same thing with me, but she died a little over two years ago. Then things began to change."

"I guess your pa didn't want much to do with you, did he?"

"His drinking never was a particularly good situation for me, but after Ma died, well..." I dropped my eyes.

Robert put his hand on my shoulder. "I've seen it all before. There's something about whiskey that can bring out the worst in some people. I tried it once. It made me sick as a dog, but I reckon some people like it or they wouldn't do it. Some folks get happy and some just get mean."

"I ain't never tried it. Pa, well, he just sort of gave me a natural inclination away from the stuff."

The sergeant came by our little fire and said we needed to check on our horses and take care of our tents. "I'm Sergeant Murphy. If you need to know anything, always ask me. I'm the mother goose around here, at least until Captain Hare decides to shift us around, which is bound to happen. I can tell you, even in the old US army, about the time things start to get comfortable, orders will change or somebody new will come along. Get used to it, boys. Take this unit...I originally signed up with Major Davis...It was Davis's Mounted Battalion, but Major Davis has been moved and now we have that Frenchman Colonel DeBray."

Robert spoke up, "Frenchman?"

"Aye," Sergeant Murphy said. "I've seen his like in the old Army. Schooled at some high fallutin' military place in France. Like a West Pointer, he is. He's a stern officer once you get past that accent of his. Saint Cyr, I think I heard the lieutenant say. Be prepared to learn a little military discipline in this outfit. I'm old army and I'm used to it, but I can tell you this will not be like the other cavalry outfits I've seen forming up since the war began."

Then he slapped me on the back and his voice took on his more official tone and said, "Now get after those horses, on the double quick!"

We both jumped up and shook the dirt out of our trousers as we ran for the small enclosure where we had tied our horses. There was an old slave tending the stockade, bringing piles of hay from a nearby wagon closer to the horses. As Robert took some fresh hay from this pile to his sorrel, this old man shoveled his way over near me.

He whispered, "Captain Jack?"

I was startled. I had never seen this man before. "Yes. Do I know you?"

"I reckon not," he said, "but ah knows you. If you need anything here, you just ask. Miss Vanita tole me how good you was to old Moze in his final days."

"You knew Moze?"

"No, sir. Just knows of him."

"So you know Vanita?"

He widened his eyes, pulled the top of his shirt over, and revealed a VV mark on his shoulder.

"She'll be watching us both. You just let me know. Ah gots eyes and ears here that can help you."

I said, "Thanks," and began tending to Elvira.

"This here's your horse? What her name?"

"Elvira," I said.

"Fine piece of horse flesh," he said. "Ah'm Jimmy. I'll keep a special eye on Elvira for you, Captain Jack."

I glanced at Robert; he hadn't heard.

"Listen, Jimmy," I whispered, "I'm a little new to army life, but I know you need to watch calling me 'captain' around here. They are a little touchy about such things."

"I'll be careful. Now you just go abouts your business."

I walked over to Robert who was finishing up with his horse. Even in the dark I could tell it was a beautiful chestnut color. "Pretty horse," I said.

"Sadie," he said. "She was a gift from my pa on my fourteenth birthday." He put his chin to his chest. "Right before he died." Then he raised his head and said, "She's my pride and joy."

I patted Sadie's neck and she looked back and snorted at the perceived interloper, but in truth, I think she liked the attention and was just showing off.

Robert pointed with his chin. "So there are slaves here? I didn't expect that, not here in the cavalry."

"I heard someone else talking about it. They reckoned some were impressed from local plantations to help set up the camp."

"You know him? He acted mighty familiar to you."

"Knew a slave I used to watch over," I lied. "Everybody seems to know of Old Moze."

"Old Moze, the hunter? I've heard of *him*. What do you mean watch over? Overseer?"

"Not as fancy as that. A slave can't rightly carry a gun, right? But the widow woman I worked for would lease him out as a guide, and like as not, he'd need to do the actual shooting. Most of the dandies we went out with couldn't hit the broad side of a barn. I'd carry the gun... and just hand it to him when it was time for the kill. He was the most amazing shot I have ever seen."

Robert's eyes were wide. "I guess I never thought about it. A slave with a gun. Land sakes. Did he teach you to hunt?"

"He tried, I guess. I learned a lot from him. Hunting, fishing, horse handling, carpentry, gardening...he had a lot of skills."

We walked back to our tent. It was dark and a cold wind was blowing. We could see the dim glow of candles from some of the other tents. Our tent was just as we left it, except someone had deposited two more blankets inside the flap; we suspected Sergeant Murphy. We spread the extra blankets on the ground and then clambered in. After fastening the flap, the effect of the wind was abated and we were already much warmer.

"We need some candles," Robert said.

"Yeah. You got any money?"

"Just a little my ma gave me when I told her I was leaving. I didn't want to take it, but she insisted."

"I have a little myself. Maybe we can find a sutler tomorrow and get some candles."

"Good idea," Robert said. "Good night, Jack."

"Sweet dreams, Robert."

"Not much chance of that," he said, laughing.

Eight

We woke before daylight to the sound of a horn blaring; it marked the rude advent of our military life. An even rougher indication emerged with the booming voice of our dear Sergeant Murphy.

"All right...fall in! That means get your lazy bones out from under those blankets. Come out here and greet this great new day with a smile! On the double quick!"

Robert and I ran out and became the first two in the line because we had slept in our clothes as an added defense against the cold. Slowly, by ones and twos, the other members of our squad stood next to us. With every minute, the sergeant's face began to gain a little more color. He became incensed at the slowness of some of the recruits. Elsewhere in the encampment we could hear the screams of other sergeants filtering through the dark. Finally we all stood in a line in front of him.

"Thank you for choosing to join me this fine morning, gentlemen. Just a word to the wise. When I say 'fall in' I mean: FALL IN!"

He scrutinized the entire column of men. "First things first. In this man's army I suggest you sleep in your clothes. There are practical considerations for this. For instance, your Yankee brethren may not have the patience to wait for you to be dressed and ready before they attack you. If you have yet to notice, this is the ARMY and we are at WAR. You've signed up and now it is time for you to put your toes on the line."

He walked up and down the column of men as he continued. "In these first few days, we will get you used to the changes that will be your new life. Understand, gentlemen, my patience with you will gradually subside. In the next few days as the company fills out, we will begin assigning more tasks. In a short time we will break camp and move to a new location. This is as much for training as for hygienic practicality. Your first order of business this morning will be tending to your horses. Without our horses we are just...*infantry* and believe me, you don't want to be infantry, not for a second. Now, I need some volunteers..." he looked right at Robert and me, "you two, front and center."

We stepped forward.

"Names?"

"Robert White."

"Jack Benson."

"White and Benson will do. You two will have the first latrine duty while the others tend to the horses. You will tend to your horses when you complete latrine duty. Understood?"

"Uh, Sergeant, what is latrine duty?" Robert asked.

"Ah, I'll show you that joy in due time. The rest of you, fall out and hop to it on the double-quick!"

It wasn't that we didn't know what a latrine was, at least in theory, but we didn't know what the duty entailed. And we didn't know where the "latrine" was. The night before, we had simply relieved ourselves nearby.

"White, Benson, follow me."

We followed the sergeant a few yards behind the line of tents to a small grove of trees where we found a deep trench.

"Ah, the joys of camp life, eh, boys? This is our squad latrine. Every time we make a new camp, we dig a new one, just for us. And every morning, we cover the previous day's leavings with a fresh layer of hay and dirt from those two piles over yonder. Simple enough? The shovels are there," he said pointing.

The stench was awful.

"Don't mind the smell, gentlemen. You'll get used to it, but of course, we are not up to full strength yet. But never you mind, I can tell you this is important to all of us. Hygiene is as vital to an army as its food. It isn't in the regulations but I tell you from experience. Even your best surgeon is not as acquainted with the intricacies of hygiene as well as a seasoned veteran of any army. Now hop to it... I like you boys, and did you a favor. This duty will get a lot worse as the days trot by, if you can excuse my little joke. This is my reward to you for being first in line this morning. Your turn will come again, but not for a while," Sergeant Murphy said with a guffaw.

Robert and I both grabbed shovels and started tossing scoops of dirt and hay across the disgusting piles of excrement.

"Not too thick, boys, we need to leave enough to last through the entire pit."

We worked our way around the trench and the entire operation took less than an hour. I wondered why one of the camp Negroes wasn't employed to this task, but then I realized this was part of our new life of Army discipline. Also, since the workers were impressed from nearby farms or plantations, they likely didn't travel with us when we were on the move, so this was solely a soldiers' duty. We just performed the task assigned to us and were grateful when it was finished.

As we returned to the duty area, we encountered one of the men approaching us.

"Y'all got things all fresh and ready for me?" It was one of the "old" recruits, who had already been in the camp the day we arrived.

"Yes," I said. "Ready for a new day."

While we were tending to our horses, the recruit we met at the latrine area approached us again. "Y'all have some nice horses," he said.

"Thanks," I said.

He stuck out his hand. "Name's Rufus, Rufus Macombe."

"I'm Jack Benson."

"Robert White."

I was curious about this seasoned soldier so I asked him, "When did you sign up?"

"Right before Christmas. December twenty-third."

"Here I was thinking you were some kind of veteran in this outfit, and you've only been here less than a week longer than me?"

"Not even that long. I got a furlough to spend a couple of days with my family for Christmas." He went back over to finish tending to his horse.

Army life was a series of routines. Get up, tend the horses, eat breakfast, then drill. The food in the early days was plentiful but did not provide much in the way of variety. Bacon or salt beef, and grits or cornmeal mush. This was how we started our days. In those early days, we still had coffee. I had not taken coffee much in my youth, but given how little else we were provided, it seemed silly to reject it. Army coffee was strong and was usually flavored with a goodly dose of sugar.

After eating, we were called to order by the sergeant, and we began to learn the next order of business in army life: drills. There was an open area next to our camp, and our squad and three others were instructed to fall in, and after a little more instruction in the proper stance and response to commands, we commenced to walk to and fro, turning or stopping according to command. In those early days, my shoes were tight and the morning dew wetted them, but this served to break them in and mold them to my feet. There was some grumbling amongst the soldiers that we were supposed to be cavalrymen. I think the sergeant heard this and he called, "HALT!"

He had us stand there for a full minute at attention, lambasting a few who broke attention to stifle a cough. Then he spoke.

"I heard some grumbling about marching when you are supposed to be cavalry. Let me tell you something. This is the army. You have to learn to follow orders. In some ways, it is the only way you have a chance of surviving in a battle. Horse or foot, you have to listen for the sound of my voice and respond instantly. THAT is what drilling is all about. I served in the old army and it was the same. Colonel DeBray served in the army in France and it was the same. It was the same for the Spartans in ancient Greece. It was the same for the Romans. It has been the same all through history. It is a soldier's right to complain but, just the same, you have to drill." He slammed a fist into his hand.

"First, we drill on foot so you learn to listen, to hear, and to instantly respond, *then* we will move to our horses. And understand, them horses are smarter than most of you, so I expect they'll learn military drill a good sight better. Now, let's get back to it, shall we?"

In the distance, we could hear the other squads similarly occupied. We marched and marched and marched until our stomachs growled. We broke for a midday meal, then we marched the rest of the day. The sergeant's previous pleasant tone took a darker turn every time we made a mistake. He cursed and called us names and expressed his regrets that our mothers had ever given birth to us.

We completed regular camp routines after drilling, and toward evening more recruits came in. The weather was milder than the previous day. Winter was like that in Houston; one day cold, one day mild, one day rain, one day not. Frost was rare, but as December moved into January, we knew we could expect more than a few days of frost.

Robert and I heard of a sutler wagon set up near one of the other companies, and after we stopped drilling for the day, we asked the sergeant if we could go procure some candles.

"Aye, boys, go get you some candles. Get a lot. The nights are long and lonely. I expect we'll be providing a few from time to time, but right now you need to go get what you can."

A sutler tent was like a small store. The owner was a shifty looking man with a waxed mustache who implied he might have other items not on display. I presumed it was most likely whiskey or rum or some such and I wasn't interested. My meagre savings was going to provide me with light to help me pass the long nights. I also spied a few dime novels, and I picked one of them up along with my supply of candles. Robert came out with more candles and some candies.

On the way back, we sauntered past the cook wagon and Robert spied some discarded cans, most likely the result of some extended rations for the officers. We enquired from the cook and he acquiesced to our request to grab a couple of the cans. We got some smaller ones to serve as makeshift candle holders. As an afterthought, I grabbed a larger can that had held some kind of meat to use as a kind of pot if we needed it. This turned out to be a grand idea as the cook tent's stock of raw materials soon diminished to almost nothing once the company began to expand in numbers.

The sergeant was a genius at keeping us busy even in our down time. His favorite pastime involved walking around and simply picking up anything that was on the ground, even twigs and acorns. He wanted the camp to be clean and neat and seemed most happy if it resembled a well-kept village square or a field recently cleared by a herd of goats.

There were other duties, too. We, of course, tended to our horses a couple of times a day. Picket duty fell to each of us in turn. It basically meant standing guard over our area of the camp, although at this stage of the war it seemed unlikely we would be molested as we slept. We had not been issued weapons yet, but were told they were coming. Until we were armed, our method of guarding in the event of an attack would be to call an alarm and hopefully overwhelm any intruders by sheer numbers.

Our second night passed much more peaceably with the addition of candlelight. Some of our camp-mates joined us, welcomed by the illumination. We talked, mostly sharing conjecture as to the progress of the war, but news was in short supply. The army, I found out, was fueled by rumor, and whenever any action was expected, the rumors would fly. Usually, the accuracy of this information would not stand the test of time.

In a few days, our weapons arrived. We were each issued some old short guns. Hall's Carbines was what the sergeant called them. I was used to a long-barreled muzzle loading weapon, but these guns were shorter than the muskets most of us were more familiar with.

As I thought on it, I realized these shorter guns would be easier to carry on horseback.

Once our squads were issued these new arms, we were instructed in their use. There was a mechanism that allowed the breach of the weapon to swing up to reveal a chamber. Charges were rolled with a ball in a wad of parchment and inserted in the chamber, and the barrel was swung up. Because of this requirement, we received more instruction in the manufacture of these shot charges.

"I know it seems hard, gentlemen, but it will help occupy some of your otherwise wasted free time. We may occasionally receive these charges pre-made, but for now, we will do it ourselves."

Most of us had never seen the likes of these guns but one of the older hands in the company, a man who had served time in the old army, said they were not new.

"I've used these many a time. They are quicker to load and surprisingly accurate once you get used to its offset gun sight."

Still, it was considered a fair cavalry weapon because of its size and the ease of loading. I was lucky. In looking down my barrel, I discovered it had been rifled. The old hand had insisted they were smooth bore, but before the war, it had been the habit of the old US army to rifle the barrels of many older arms. I remembered Moze telling me about the effect of rifling. I swear, he always surprised me with the things he knew. I didn't know a slave could be so schooled in general knowledge.

"See them grooves cut in the barrel?" he had told me once while he was showing me how to clean the gun.

"Yes, I see them."

"Them's the things what grabs that old bullet and puts it to spin. Spinning is God's way of making it go true to the target. Makes it go farther, too. Don't ask me how, I don't know, but it works."

I smiled as I remembered this and felt very fortunate to have received a rifled version. In the days to come, a small area was set aside for practice, and various squads of Company K took a turn familiarizing ourselves with the operation of these weapons. I took to it like a duck to water, and the sergeant was amazed at how I could fire several shots in quick succession, always hitting the bottles and cans we were using as targets.

"Good shooting, boy," the sergeant had told me. He had taken a special liking to Robert and me, and one day, he told us he knew we were younger than we had said, it was obvious to him. But he also told us we were two of his best men.

"You follow orders and are keen to learn. I like that in a soldier."

These Hall's rifles had an attached ring, at least some of them did, and we were also instructed in ways to attach them to our saddles in a manner that left our hands free most of the time. We could still quickly detach them and bring them to bear if needed. Some of them also had a bayonet that could slide out, but it was of little use to a horse soldier.

Soon, we started drilling with our horses as well, and as the camp began to take on more recruits, we started to have the look and feel of a real army. Now that we were becoming more adept at drills, both on foot and on horseback, Robert and I became comfortable with army life. We began to see more of the officers during our drills, and one day, Colonel DeBray himself came to watch us, both on foot and on horseback. He seemed impressed and even endeavored to issue a few commands to us in his distinctive accent. He conferred with a major and some of the lieutenants, who shared some minor concerns with the sergeant. Captain Hare was away trying to secure more recruits. The company now had about seventy souls ready to serve Texas and the Confederate States.

Nine

Sergeant Murphy came to us with some exciting news. "We are now ready to do some real soldiering."

We had endured daily drills for weeks, both on foot and on our horses, and we were all excited for the opportunity to go out into the field as true cavalry. The sergeant appointed a corporal and hand-picked the members of the squad. Being as Robert and I were a couple of his favorites, he gave us the honor of accompanying the first patrol. Our friend Rufus was in the group of nine as well.

As we saddled our mounts, we could tell they were excited because horses instinctively know when something is up. Like us, they were weary of the monotonous drills and were anxious to get out and stretch their legs.

When everything was ready, we formed into a group with Corporal May in the lead. We all rode behind him, in two columns of four. Our carbines were slung on the sides of our saddles. I imagine we were a resplendent sight in the early morning light, with the sun glinting off the yellow stripes on our trouser legs. Our lines were straight and we moved in unison.

Our intent was to head west to the Brazos River and to follow it down to the Gulf of Mexico, then patrol down the coast for a few days before returning. We had rolled up our blankets and what supplies we could muster. We greatly hoped to depend on the kindness of citizens to help supplement our larder. I had yet to demonstrate my hunting skills, but I knew I could provide game if need be. This, like the drills, was considered a training mission.

As we traveled, curious citizens would stop and watch us, and it made us feel important. Young boys were the best spectators, as nothing excites a young boy more than the sight of soldiers on the move. They would yip and holler, following up with a hearty wave, jumping up and down with obvious delight. We would wave and offer salutations where appropriate. Young ladies would turn away then cock their heads back to catch our eyes, then suddenly avert their faces again, as if to avoid the spell of a dashing young man in uniform.

We encountered long stretches of open land as we followed a road toward the southwest, hoping to intersect with the village of Bailey's Prairie, then continue on to the southwest until we reached the river. In the early afternoon, we reached the village where some grateful citizens thrust portions of bread and butter into our hands as we rode along. Others added cloth bags filled with fruit and jerky, all of which we gratefully accepted because we were hungry. We did not stop to eat, but we did pause to water our horses and allow them to graze.

Not long after resuming our march, we knew we were in the river bottoms of the Brazos and found a path we thought would generally follow the river to the southeast. The Brazos is a lazy meandering waterway, full of soggy swamp areas, but the weather was cool so we were not much bothered by bugs.

As we approached more farmsteads, dogs would consider us to be intruders and would bark continuously. The farmers would come out to see what the fuss was about, and most of them would yup and holler, waving us on our way. Some would just stand and stare. Although most people favored secession, some were still unionists. The latter prospect was not a popular stand to take in these early days of the war, so they would pretty much keep to themselves.

As the afternoon wore into the early stretches of evening, we could smell salt air and thus knew we were close to our objective. We often caught brief glimpses of the serene river. Soon the path we were following crossed a road of sorts. I suppose it was also more of a path.

"I know this road," Rufus said to the corporal. "I think it will take us down to the shoreline."

We took his advice and followed it. It led away from the river to the east, northeast and in a short while, just as the sun was setting, we could hear the ocean and knew we had reached our objective. Beyond a series of salt marshes, we could see the outline of small dunes.

We had no tents on this trip, just oilcloth and blankets. There was a cold wind blowing off the Gulf. Several of us foraged up and down the beach and retrieved enough dry driftwood to make us a nice fire. The thought of a fire was good, but in practice, we found it hard to achieve because we could not find sufficient kindling. One of our group, William Parrott, had a substantial Bowie knife, which he used in the guise of a hatchet to hack off small slivers of some of the pieces of driftwood until he had a small pile of kindling. The rest of us huddled around the makeshift fire pit we had dug in the drier inland-facing sand to block the wind until Rufus managed to start this kindling to burning. We nibbled at our sparse rations of jerked meat and bread. We decided to save the fruit for the morning.

The horses were secured; they nibbled at the salt grass but did not care much for it. We had refilled our canteens at a well not far up the road and had watered our horses there, so we did not worry much for their health at this point. Rufus warned us away from the brackish water closer to the coast, but we had noted a shallow fresh water pond about a half mile inland.

Our plan was to set watches for the night then to patrol several miles up the coast to the east from this point. It was known that Union blockaders would sometimes come in close and send shore parties to secure water and supplies, and we all hoped we would have the opportunity to engage some interlopers. I don't think Corporal May was quite as keen on that idea as some of us were. Robert and I volunteered for the first watch, and we set to gather more wood before the others closed their eyes. Robert had a nice timepiece and it would serve to remind us when it was time to wake our relief.

Night watch was long and lonely, but we chatted much the same as we did every night in our tent. We took turns feeding the fire to fend off the chill. The sound of the waves crashing against the shore made the night seem ever more peaceful and reminded me of nighttime adventures I used to enjoy along the shore as a child in Galveston.

Occasionally I would stand on the dunes and imagine I could see the lights of ships, but such glimpses were so fleeting I concluded that perhaps I was seeing a reflection of the stars. At one point, I looked up and saw the moon would be full in a few days, and I was reminded of Vanita's instruction to leave my trick bag in the light of the full moon. I had almost forgotten this in the rush of new experiences. I fingered the bag in my trouser pocket and plotted how to place it in secret. I assumed I'd be able to find a safe spot while visiting the latrine and then retrieve it the same way. I contemplated the bag's power while sitting by the fire, casually rubbing the marked area on my shoulder.

When our two hours was up, we roused the next two victims for their own singular stint of army torture. We sought out our oil cloth beds and covered ourselves in our blankets to shiver the rest of the night away. I woke to the sounds of our tiny camp stirring and realized volunteering for the first watch was a good thing, as it guaranteed a lengthy uninterrupted sleep. I scanned the horizon looking for scant reminders of the elusive lights, but decided they had been a mirage. We had no breakfast to speak of except for the fruit given to us by the citizens we had passed. The horses were restless, so we doused our fire with seawater and mounted up.

We were tired and had no coffee, but the fruit was a welcome breakfast. After taking the horses to the small pond for some water and letting them graze for a while, we returned to the ocean and followed the beach. The quiet loneliness of the winter morning beach was both beautiful and sad. At times like this, I missed the companionship of Moze. We were all tired, hungry, and miserable, and I for one was glad our sergeant was not there to tighten up our line as we continued on our mission.

The only invaders on this chilly January morning were gulls who kept pace with us as we walked along. I don't think the horses cared much for walking on the sand, but they were surely thankful, as we were, that the weather was mild. We heard a steam whistle somewhere far away, which we supposed must be from either a nearby riverboat or one of the blockaders. It might have perhaps been a locomotive because it was faint and quite distant. Corporal May stopped our march for a moment so we could listen, but after one brief blast, the sound never returned.

After several miles, we spied a track heading off inland. Rufus again thought he recognized it.

"Corporal May, I think this path will take us back inland where we can intersect with a road that will take us on toward our camp."

The corporal agreed and we headed inland after stopping one more time to scour the horizon for any of the Union boats.

Not far up this trail, we encountered a farmhouse where I could swear I caught a whiff of bacon and coffee. I imagined my hunger had heightened my sense of smell.

"Jack, dismount and enquire if we might water our horses here and let them graze a moment."

I complied and cautiously knocked on the door.

An old woman answered my knock with the barrel of an ancient shotgun.

"Whut cho want? Is you Yankees?"

"No'm," I said. "We're with the Twenty-sixth Texas Cavalry, on patrol."

She poked her head out and surveyed our group.

"Whut cho want?"

The corporal moved his horse forward. "Sorry to disturb you, ma'am. We wondered if you would let our horses tarry a few minutes to graze and take some fresh water."

She looked us up and down again. "So youze Texas troops? "

"Yes, ma'am," Corporal May said. "Confederate Cavalry."

She smiled, showing a few gaps in her teeth. "Good. Got no stomach for no more Yankees coming about. You boys hungry?"

I think everyone's mouth watered at hearing this simple question, but Corporal May greatly disappointed us by replying, "We have rations, ma'am...we wouldn't want to impose too much."

"Shucks, ain't no imposition. My stove is hot and I can whip up some biscuits before you can shake a stick. Got bacon, too. Since my boy joined up, I've got more than I kin eat, and it's good somebody can eat it afore it gets spoilt."

"What unit is he in?"

"Don't rightly know. Don't know if'n I'll ever since he can't read or write."

The corporal dismounted. "What's his name?"

"Will Beasley. Nineteen years old. He left me alone here, but I can take care of myself. You boys want coffee? Can make me a new pot, but I've only got one other cup asides from mine."

"Mrs. Beasley, we would gladly share."

Everyone dismounted at this point.

I spoke up, "Ma'am, do you need any chores done around here while we wait? We could perhaps repay you with work."

"I can split the wood but it hurts my back. If you boys don't mind, maybe split me a mess of wood?"

I motioned to Robert and Rufus, and we all headed over to a nearby wood pile. By the time the corporal called us, we had split quite a quantity of wood for her, and we carried several armloads to the house when we returned.

We each wolfed down a warm biscuit stuffed with a thick and crisp slab of the best bacon I've ever tasted. The coffee was bitter but heavily sweetened, and I relished the few sips of it I managed before Rufus grabbed the cup out of my hands for his turn.

Corporal May said, "Boys, we better mount up and be on our way."

"You boys be safe and come back. I don't need no more marauding Yankees coming around 'chere."

This was the second time she had made this statement, and the corporal spoke up.

"So you've seen Yankees here?"

"From one o' them ships out yonder in the Gulf," she said, "looking for water mostly. They offered to pay me for drawing a couple of barrels worth from mah well. About drained it dry for the day. I told them their Yankee greenbacks was worthless to me, so they gave me a danged paper voucher and told me to cash it in after they won the war. I spit on the ground at that point and they left."

"May I see the voucher?"

"Sure," she said and disappeared back inside. She returned with a wrinkled bit of paper.

Corporal May surveyed the note and looked back at us. "Our patrol is a success, men. This is proof the Yankees have come ashore here." He turned back to Mrs. Beasley. "Mrs. Beasley, may I have this note to show to my superiors? There have been rumors of the Yankees landing around here, but we had no proof. Colonel DeBray will be very interested in seeing this evidence."

"Take it. If it helps our country in the fight for this here war, then I'm happy to be rid of it."

Corporal May tipped his cap. "Ma'am, we are eternally in your debt. Thank you so much for your hospitality. "

She watched us as we rode down the track. We eventually met up with a road Rufus knew would take us back toward Houston. I knew it, too, because I had spied the faint outline of a double V on a tree at the crossroads.

We encountered citizens again on our return trip and, just as before, people either waved and whooped or ignored us as they saw fit. We arrived at our encampment toward the end of daylight and unsaddled our horses.

A while later, Corporal May sought out several of us and said, "Captain Hare and Colonel DeBray were very pleased with the results of our patrol."

Ten

In the weeks after the patrol, our company had expanded to its full rank of about a hundred souls. Drills continued, and we worked hard to indoctrinate the newer recruits in the ways of our unit. Rumors circulated that we were bound for any number of far off places. They seemed to be fighting this war every place except Texas.

One day Rufus told us, "I hear General Albert Sidney Johnston is commanding a big army in Mississippi."

Robert countered, "I hear it's New Orleans that is in peril."

General Johnston was well known in Texas, so if I was going to be heading any place in particular, I wanted to go join him. Visions of battle and glory floated in the background of all our minds. This was further bolstered by the fact that supplies were being stockpiled in each company, and almost every day, orders were issued to prepare equipment. We were being instructed in the ways and means of breaking a camp, loading wagons, and getting packed for a march quickly and in good order.

One day we were informed New Orleans had indeed fallen to the Union and we would not be heading east as yet. Our disappointment was great, but within a very few days, we received word that we, along with another detachment of cavalry, would be heading to the west instead. General Sibley had taken a large force to New Mexico and he needed reinforcements. It was not quite as exciting as the expected march to the east. The prospect of crossing a wide, desolate expanse seemed a daunting notion to most of us.

In fact, one of the newer recruits, Adam Huffman, had traveled with his father to El Paso just a year earlier.

"I'll tell you this. There is nothing out there but rattlesnakes, rocks, and scrubland. Water will be hard to come by. Even in the spring it will be terribly hot. Both us and the animals will suffer."

A few days later, we received our orders and began our first march as a brigade. Our instruction had been excellent, and we broke camp just as we had been taught. The latrine pits were filled and the wagons were packed. We wrapped our personal kits into efficient horse packs, and we were soon on the march. Our lines were straight and no one straggled. Colonel DeBray's insistence that we drill every day had forged us into a formidable-looking outfit on the march.

It was the first time I ever left the flat coastal area, and as we moved west, I marveled at the hills we encountered. We again attracted a lot of interest every time we passed anyone, whether it was another traveler or a settlement.

The people of Texas grandly supported their protectors, or at least most of them did. From time to time, we spied dwellings we knew were inhabited by the wisps of smoke coming out of their chimneys, but no one came out to greet us. As we proceeded through harsher landscapes to the west, the welcoming gifts of food became much rarer.

Scouts were sent ahead of the columns to find suitable camps for the night, and when we approached the sites these scouts had chosen, we would quickly create comfortable but temporary outposts. If sufficient timber existed, we would erect corrals, but often we had to be satisfied with using rope for this purpose. Work details dug shallow latrine trenches and gathered firewood in quantities sufficient for our use. Although our tents and other bulky equipment were carried in a wagon train that travelled behind our main column, in mild weather we rarely resorted to the tents. We generally stretched out on the ground with our blankets.

Riding on the march is tiring work and sleep generally came readily to us, but such slumber was regularly interrupted by the chore of picket duty. On a march like this, we needed a goodly number of pickets, so more of us were enlisted to the duty than at our more permanent camp. We were spread out so the time was spent in lonely isolation.

We were several days' march out of San Antonio when a rider caught up to us.

"Sibley's expedition has gone bust! He's returning to Texas."

Sergeant Murphy told us, "Our orders have changed. We are headed to a place near the San Bernard River."

Since this was some miles west of Houston, we executed what was called in military terms a counter-march, meaning we turned around and retraced our steps. In our case, we felt some measure of defeat at the notion of being once again deprived of our chance at battlefield glory.

We were grateful for one thing, though. It was good to be getting back to more populous and prosperous regions where we could enjoy the generosity of the citizens of our great state. Beeves and hogs were donated to the cause, along with bags of cornmeal and what other provisions citizens could spare. We finally reached our destination and created, as best as we could, a more permanent encampment following the same general plan we had used outside Houston. We kept quite busy with our normal routines. A military camp is like a small city, and there is always some chore that needs to be performed; regular patrols were sent out as well.

Daily drills commenced and quite often people would come over from the several communities nearby under the guise of augmenting our supplies, but they would tarry a while and watch us drill with great interest. Our uniforms had become quite a mishmash of styles and colors because, as the brigade had grown, the supply of uniforms had diminished. Kind ladies of nearby towns formed aid societies, and together they would create quite serviceable outfits for us from donated curtains and blankets and what other fabrics they could find.

The local interest was so great, Colonel DeBray began to hold regular parades to replace some of our drills, and we would show off our skill for those citizens as a reward for their efforts on our behalf. We were proud to do it, although for us it was extra duty.

The citizens would come to our parades dressed in their Sunday finest, riding in their carriages in grand style. When they saw us in our wild assortment of colors and styles, they took to calling us "The Menagerie," and we accepted this term as a compliment. We would sometimes use it amongst ourselves as well. We were indeed a colorful and unlikely group when on parade, but our superior marching style was evident even beyond the look of our fanciful exterior.

One day, I was sent on an errand for the quartermaster. My orders were to retrieve some promised steers from a local plantation. I was sent alone because it was known I had some reputation as an overseer. This was likely because I had told one or two people of my employment with Mrs. Jenkins. There are no secrets in an army camp beyond the confines of one's own lips.

I was to take charge of about four slaves who would help me drive the cattle back to our camp. I was uncomfortable with the task because I knew I was no overseer. Old Moze had let me know from the first day who was in charge. But the unit needed the meat and the captain had decided I was the one to go and get it, so I strove to be a good soldier and follow my orders. At least I had some minor experience with handling one cow.

A stern-faced plantation owner showed me the stock he was providing, about ten stout steers, and pointed out the four black figures who were to accompany me. I did not see any mounts for them.

"Won't they have horses?"

The man laughed heartily and then said, "You must not be from around here. No, they will walk along. They're good boys, and they know what to do. They'll behave for you or they know what will happen to them. You boys understand?"

The largest responded, "Yassuh, we won't cause no trouble."

I didn't quite understand how this would work, but the four men seemed to know what they needed to do. They spread themselves out and surrounded the animals, shooing them along on foot. Not a one of them had shoes. I followed behind the group on Elvira.

They stretched out their hands when they needed to and called out to any steer showing an inclination to change direction, keeping them in line with a skill that was impressive to me. They even had a name for each one of them and would coax them along with either a calm word or an insult. The steers responded well and it was just a few miles to the encampment, so we were soon there and the beeves were handed over for their intended use.

It was getting along about noon, so I asked the biggest of the group, "Did you bring anything to eat?"

"Nosuh," he said.

I went to one of the cooks and asked if I might have a little something to feed my charges and at first he sneered at me. But after he looked beyond me and saw my hungry crew, he relented.

"I've got some fatback you can have and there are scraps of cornbread left from the last mess."

He put these together in a cloth grain sack and handed it to me.

"Thank you."

"Slaves or no slaves, they's got to eat I guess...and they helped you with the steers."

I refilled my canteen from the cook's water barrel. "They worked hard."

The four slaves started back, with me following slowly on Elvira.

A mile or so from the camp, I informed them of what I had in the sack and they seemed most grateful. We stopped under the shade of a huge oak tree, and they gathered a small quantity of fallen timber and helped me start us a fire. I used my knife to cut the fatback into five chunks, and we each impaled a piece on a stick and held it over the fire until it got toasty. The cornbread was divided up and both items were heartily devoured.

I opened my canteen and took a swig and handed it to the big man.

He shook his head. "Nosuh," he said.

"You've just walked miles in the hot sun, you must be thirsty. You need to wash down that cornbread or it will stick in your throat."

The man looked all around as if to make sure no one could see and he meekly took a drink. I motioned to the rest of them and they each very sheepishly took their turn with the canteen.

"Thank you, suh," was the reply from the big man. They all seemed genuinely afraid. "Suh, may I ask your name?"

"Jack Benson," I said.

The largest man gasped and the last man dropped the canteen. They all exchanged wild-eyed glances and then stared at me, a visual chorus of wide eyes and open mouths.

I was trying to get the stopper back in the canteen before the contents were completely lost when the big man said with an astonished tone, "Is you *Captain* Jack?"

All four appeared to be in shock. I guess I was, too. "Where did you hear that?" I asked.

"S-S-Suh, ah don't rightly know, I first got the notion after a hag-riding fit. I think we...all of us...did, so we just knowed. I had my suspicions maybe you was the Captain Jack we been expectin', but after you give me your canteen, I was sure it was you."

I was speechless.

"Let me ask you, if you really Captain Jack, yo gots the mark?" He pulled down a corner of his shirt and showed me a fresh, crimson-tinged VV mark on his shoulder. "I remembers the witch saying I should look for the mark."

Again I was speechless. I gingerly pulled my shirt open and revealed my shoulder. They all gasped again then reached out and each in turn touched my arm like I was some kind of specter sent by the almighty.

"We best be getting back, Captain Jack. We sho appreciates your kindnesses, suh. We knowed you wuz coming sometime or other, just didn't know it was today."

"What are your names?"

Again, the big man seemed surprised but responded, "I'ze Big Jim, dat's Levi, Caleb, and he's Little Jim."

I remounted and said, "Well, Big Jim, let's head down the road."

"Yes, Captain."

"Please, just call me Jack. The army is a bit touchy on that 'captain' stuff when a soldier isn't an officer."

"Yes, suh," he said. Then he gently reached out and touched my leg, "And, suh, if yo needs any help while you hereabouts, you just send word for Big Jim. It'll get to me and I'll help with wut I can."

"I'll do that." I mounted Elvira and we all proceeded down the road.

The stern man was waiting for us at the gate to his place.

"Where have you been? I expected you half an hour ago."

"We stopped to eat some fatback and cornbread," I said.

"I didn't send no food. They eats when I feed them."

This statement seemed to get my dander up because I didn't take to kindly to the notion of withholding food from anybody. Perhaps I was emboldened by my uniform and new station in life, but I decided to let him know how I felt about the matter.

I leaned forward from my saddle. "Listen, mister, I don't know how you run your men down here, but up where I'm from, we *feed* people else we don't get the work we expect out of them. So I got them something to eat. You got a problem with that?"

The man was noticeably flustered, perhaps embarrassed by the connotation that he didn't know how to run his own slaves.

"No, I guess not." Then I think he decided to turn it back on me. "They didn't give you no trouble, did they?"

But I was ready for him.

"Not at all. Like I told you, I know how to run *my* men." I winked at Big Jim and he ever so gently nodded back as I spun Elvira around, gave her a gentle touch from my spurs, and galloped off back down the lane.

Eleven

A few days after the incident with the plantation owner, I was ordered to accompany another squad to the coast, with Sergeant Fant commanding the patrol. At the time, a number of our soldiers were down with measles, but I was okay because I had already suffered through a bout with them a few years before.

We assembled our equipment and soon headed toward the coast. The detail contained eight men in addition to the sergeant. I had seen a number of these men around the camp but was not very familiar with them. We chatted amicably as we ambled down the road. One who looked Mexican rode alongside me. He looked a bit older than me, perhaps thirty or so.

"I'm Jack Benson," I said.

"Ricardo Zavala," he said, "but most here call me Ricky." He spoke with a slight accent.

"Where you from?"

He stared at me for a moment, as if I'd asked a stupid question. "Anahuac, just to the east of Houston on the Trinity. My family has lived there since long before the revolution. My uncle fought at San Jacinto under General Houston."

I could tell I had offended him and offered my apology. "Sorry, it was a stupid question," I said. "My family lived in Galveston, but I've been living in Houston for a couple of years."

He bowed his head and we rode on in silence. Finally he spoke again. "The other fellows say you've been on one of these patrols before."

"Yes, a few weeks before we broke the old camp and went on our wild goose chase out west."

"Did you see any action?"

"Not really. But we did talk to an old lady who said she had been raided by a blockade shore party."

"Really?"

"Well, maybe not specifically raided, but some Yankees had definitely landed and come inland looking for fresh water."

"Perhaps we will be so lucky. This marching and drilling and useless traveling to nowhere... it is not why I joined this army."

"I know. I heard General Johnston's army is on the move north."

"*Si*, I have heard this rumor as well. General Johnston is a good man. My uncle befriended him in the early days of the Republic."

Everyone knew he was a long-time soldier who had served both the Republic of Texas and the US Army.

"I hear he is one of the highest ranking generals in our army."

Ricky was fingering a rosary as he rode, quietly mouthing prayers as we traveled. He noticed me glancing at him and said, "Oh, I am just saying my prayers because it is Holy Week. Are you a member of the church?"

I shook my head. "My mother raised me Methodist."

"Ah," he said. "My priest would call you a heretic, but in my experience, most Methodists seem almost more Christian than many who practice in my church. Their method of sending preachers far and wide keeps many in the faith. As for me, I see us all as brothers in Christ our Lord."

"Me, too." I did not have the heart to tell him I had not seen the inside of a church since my mother died.

This first part of our journey was much the same as my first patrol. We were given supplies as we rode, including biscuits, fried chicken, fruit, and jerky. One old codger even offered us a jug, which Sergeant Fant declined.

"Against regulations," he said.

This prompted several of our group to complain under their breath, something the sergeant ignored.

We were headed to a place called Lavaca, and it was a longer trek than the one I had taken earlier. We camped one night along the way, and the sergeant had to make numerous inquiries to keep us on the correct roads. We finally found a huge stretch of open water, but a local told us it was a bay, not the Gulf. We knew we were close because the air smelled of salt.

The sergeant consulted a map as we followed the contour of the bay. The only beings we saw were gulls, who would follow us for a while hoping for a handout, but as we had no food to spare, they would soon glide off in pursuit of other opportunities.

We eventually made our way around a spit of land connected to the coast and camped for the night just behind a series of dunes. There was a long stretch of sand beyond these dunes before one got to the ocean. Ricky and I drew the first watch. A steady wind blew off the Gulf, and the sound of the surf kept us company.

We chatted against the boredom, and he told me that, despite his family's history of loyalty to Texas, the United States, and now the Confederacy, he was distrusted because of his ancestry.

"It is not fair, Jack. Not a man here has family who fought at San Jacinto, but I do. Yet I am seen as something different because they see me as Mexican. I'm more Texan than any of them. My family has lived here for over a hundred years!"

I agreed with him. "People get odd notions in their heads, Ricky. I'm just fifteen, but I've seen it even in my short life. I deal with people based on what I see and what I know."

He gently patted my shoulder. "You are wise beyond your years, my friend."

We scanned the horizon and tried to stay awake. It was a dark night, and it was deathly quiet except for the relentless wind and the droning of the waves beating against the shore. It was close to the end of our watch when I heard a mechanical sound I remembered quite well from my days of prowling around the docks as a boy. It was the workings of a ship's steam engine.

"Did you hear something?"

Ricky was standing up and straining to see through the dark. "Of course I heard something. What is it?"

"Sounds like the steam engine on a ship," I said.

We both knew sound carried easily over the water and the blowing wind could play tricks on the ears. We watched and waited, but the sound abated.

Then, all of a sudden, I heard the faint sounds of metal against metal.

"I think that's the sound of an anchor being lowered," I said.

"*Si.*" A few minutes later we heard more sounds and then a rhythmic splash.

"Oars," Ricky whispered.

"I hear it."

"Go wake the sergeant," he said.

I ran toward a loud snoring sound. "Sergeant, Sergeant," I said, nudging him slightly.

He grumbled himself awake, and grabbed me by my shirt and pulled me close to his face.

"Wha— what...is it my watch already?"

"No, Sergeant. We heard something. We think it is a shore party."

Hearing that, he snapped himself awake and said, "Show me."

We returned to Ricky.

"Good night for something like this," I said. "There is no moon."

Sergeant Fant squinted into the wind. "I'm sure they planned it that way."

We could just make out the dark image of a boat in the water and heard vague splashes in rhythm as it moved forward. I lifted my weapon but the sergeant put his hand on the barrel and moved it down.

"Don't be hasty, Jack. We need to be sure."

We waited for several minutes and pretty soon we became aware of voices, indistinct at first, but then we began to hear what they were saying.

"How much farther is it?"

"I can't tell. Not far, I imagine."

The accents were definitely not Southern.

The sergeant went to wake the rest of the squad. "Stay here," he said before he left. "Wait for the rest of us."

We heard the sound of wood scraping against sand as they grounded into the shore. Then we heard faint splashes as the men in the boat jumped over, and more scraping as they pulled their craft to a more secure spot. We heard barrels being unloaded. I remembered the sound from my youth; an empty barrel makes a very distinctive impression on the ears.

The sergeant returned. "They must be in search of fresh water." He chuckled. "They couldn't have picked a worse spot."

It was almost as if one of the interlopers had heard him. "I tell you there won't be any water here. I know places like this...beyond those dunes it is probably a salt marsh. Fresh water will be a long hike inland."

"The captain told us to look here."

There seemed to be four of them, with two barrels.

"Wait until they get the barrels off," the sergeant whispered. "Weapons at the ready?"

We all whispered in the affirmative.

I knew we were at the extreme range of the Hall's carbines, and I could barely make out vague outlines of men in the dark shadows.

The sergeant whispered again, "Boys, let's fire a volley at them and see if we can show them they can't land here."

I had never fired a gun at a human being before. In fact, Old Moze had told me to never do it unless I was in mortal danger.

"A gun is a marvelous invention for putting food in a man's belly," he had told me, *"but it can do a powerful lot of harm to somebody. I don't take kindly to the notion of using it to inflict harm on a person, unless maybe to save your own life."*

I wondered if this was one of those times as I bore down on the shadows, using a trick Moze had taught me about shooting at night.

"When it's dark, you needs to look to the side of your target because that somehow makes you see it clear."

I was still undecided about killing, so I was nervous and my finger was lightly tapping at the trigger. My heart was racing, but I remembered what Moze told me the first time I aimed at a big deer: *"Force yourself to slow your breathing and it will help you calm yourself down. Squeeze the trigger as you breathe out the last time."*

I followed this advice as I tried to focus on one of the looming shapes I thought was probably a barrel.

"Give them the lead, boys!"

I exhaled and pulled the trigger and the Halls exploded with a tongue of flame. Only four of us fired. I think some just couldn't do it. Maybe in the excitement they had not loaded or did not have a percussion cap set right. I heard one man shriek from the shoreline and a horrible sound it was, too. I don't think I hit the man, since I heard wood splinter and assumed my shot had hit the barrel.

We heard shouting, "We've been spotted, shove off," and then the sound of wood on sand again reached us.

I was already reloaded but I think the other boys had just fired and stared into the dark.

"Fire again, Sergeant?"

"Huh?" He sounded surprised at the notion then regained his own composure. "Yes, good boy, Jack, fire at will."

I aimed at the side of the small boat, exhaled and squeezed again. The sound of wood splintering reached me. Another shot rang out from our side, and in a few seconds, I was already reloaded and fired again. I was thankful the Halls could be reloaded quickly. Just then, a flash of flame erupted from the boat, and for an instant, we could see our targets plain as day.

The shot didn't go anywhere, but my next shot was true. I hit the wooden side of the boat once again. Now the splashes were almost frantic, but their comrades had heard the commotion and were intent on a counterattack. We saw a flash from farther out on the water revealing the outline of the steamer. Somebody on board had shot at us. It was much closer than we had imagined it might be.

"We need to spread out," I said, "to give them no certain target."

"Good idea, Jack. Everyone move along the dunes!"

I figured the boat was out of my range but fired again anyway. Then I moved to the right about twenty paces. A sharpshooter on the boat had apparently taken note of my position, and just as I moved from my spot, a puff of sand popped up right where I had been situated. I turned and fired again, even though I knew it was useless as it was too far away, then I rolled further down the line only to see another puff of sand right from where I had been. I knew a good Enfield rifled musket had a far greater range than these Halls.

"Sharpshooter," I whispered.

The sergeant simultaneously realized this same fact and said, "Hold your fire, boys. They are out of our range, but they can find us by the flashes."

We continued to hear frantic splashes as they rowed back to their ship. We could see a faint glow from the smokestack as the sailors began to stoke the boiler. They wanted to be ready to go full steam and move further away from us as soon as they boarded their crew.

"They want to get away from us, probably scared we might have a cannon. I wish we did."

We heard the bumps and scrapes as they retrieved their boat and then heard the sounds of the paddles trying to gain purchase on the water. All evidence of the ship soon drifted away.

The sergeant sat down hard on the sand and let out a deep sigh followed by, "Good work, boys."

We were all panting but relieved. The excitement of the action had set our hearts to pumping. I realized I was trembling. I didn't know if this was from excitement or fear, but I soon decided to admit it was probably a little of both. The puff of sand after I first got up from my vantage point gave me a sobering lesson. I realized that not only could we shoot at the Yankees, they could, and would, shoot back.

We resumed our watch schedule, but I do not think any of us got much sleep the rest of the night. In the morning, we were all up as soon as there was enough light to see, and we went down to the shoreline. There were two weathered empty barrels standing on the shore. One of the barrels sported a splintered hole two inches below the rim. Several of the men rolled the barrels over the dunes out of sight from the water. We also spied a stain of blood in the sand, and next to that was a brand new Enfield rifled musket.

"Sergeant," Ricky said, "I think the musket should go to young Jack here. I think he fired more effectively than the rest of us."

The sergeant was admiring the prize and looked over at me. "Well, it is up to the captain to decide, but Jack can certainly take charge of it right now."

He handed me the weapon and I was speechless. It was beautiful. But I also knew it was a dubious honor as it would be bulky to carry on the rest of the patrol and I had no percussion caps or Minié balls for it. Ricky helped me secure it to my saddle, and after a cold breakfast of jerky and hard crackers, we continued our patrol.

The rest of our trip was uneventful, and we returned to the camp with our prize and our fresh war stories. It was truly our first taste of the real war, and every single one of us was elated by the experience.

Twelve

When we returned, Colonel DeBray personally commended our patrol for our effort. The sergeant was awarded the Enfield, but he declined and asked the colonel to give it to me instead. Colonel DeBray was somewhat surprised at this request, but after conferring with Captain Hare, he handed me the weapon and said he would see what he could do to procure suitable ammunition for it.

Such distinction can be a good thing, but in any group of men, there are those who will take offense to this type of recognition. Corporal AJ Dunham was such a man. Dunham was a good soldier, but he had a taste for whiskey and a quick temper. Our camp was a fair distance away from any towns of distinction and our discipline was high, but he had a knack for finding spirits, no matter our location. One night he caught me alone coming back from the latrine trench.

It was a full moon and I had just hidden my trick bag as instructed by the old woman. I don't think he observed my actions, but I did wonder if its protective power was at a minimum. Dunham emerged from the shadows, and I could smell the telltale stench of whiskey on his breath.

"Benson! Trying to get on DeBray's good side, eh? Think yer somethin' special?"

I tried to brush past him without a word. I had learned one lesson from dealing with my father: there was no use in arguing with someone under the influence. He reached out as I passed and grabbed my shoulder. I turned around to face him.

"I'll show you what we do to fancy pants around here," he said, and he took a swing at me.

I tried to dodge the blow as best as I could, but he caught me a glancing blow on the side of my head. I didn't realize it at that moment, but Lieutenant Blalock was nearby and heard the beginnings of the commotion. The blow had thrown Dunham off balance and he had fallen.

"Hey, you men there, attention!"

I followed our drill procedure and stood erect. The corporal scrambled to his feet but had trouble standing at attention due to his inebriated state.

"What goes on here?" The lieutenant's voice was strong and harsh. "You, Dunham, why did you strike this man?" Then he caught a whiff of the whiskey on Dunham's breath. "You've been drinking? In camp? Man, are you insane? This is unacceptable."

He turned to me, "Private, are you all right?"

"Yes, sir."

"Corporal, you were clearly at fault here. What is your explanation?"

I managed a quick glance at Dunham, who was swaying slightly. From the shocked look on his face, he was obviously full of the type of remorse a person gets when they've been caught dead to rights.

"No excuse, sir." His voice was still slurred by the whiskey.

"Private, you may go about your business. Corporal, we are reporting to the captain."

"Sir, may I speak?" I said.

"Yes, Private?"

"He didn't hurt me none. A lot of the fellows have been a bit jealous of me being recognized by the colonel for the last patrol. I think he just let some things get the better of him."

Corporal Dunham shot me a look of surprise.

"I appreciate your candor, Private. Still, being drunk in camp is a serious infraction." He looked right at Dunham. "I will concentrate on your drunkenness in my report to the captain, understood, Corporal?"

"Yes, sir."

In truth, I didn't much care what happened to him, but I did not want him bearing a further grudge against me. Another thing I had learned in camp and in my short life was that the less ill will a person attracts, the smoother their situation.

"Treats people the way you wishes they would treat you," Moze *had told me one time.*

As I learned the next day, Dunham was stripped of his rank and was now a private. Whenever I encountered him in later months, he never bore a further grudge against me and even thanked me once for not making his plight worse.

~ * ~

The drudgery of army life continued unabated with drills and patrols continuing to be the main attraction. Soon we were on the march again, and we moved to a new camp closer to Houston. Colonel DeBray and the quartermaster were masterminds at procuring equipment and supplies, which were always in great demand. We were fortunate in many ways because Texas, being on the edge of the country, had a border with Mexico. It allowed goods from England and other places to more easily bypass the Federal blockade. The Federals did their best to thwart these efforts, and the distances were great, but such trade served us to some advantage.

Our coastal patrols grew more frequent, and one day I was fortunate to be included in a patrol traveling to my old home town of Galveston. We secured passage on a small ferry. It ran passengers and horses from the mainland to the island. Our orders were to pass through the city and head across the western beaches to San Luis Pass and then patrol for a few days back and forth along that stretch of the coast. Such patrols were old hat now, and we performed our duty according to our training and experience.

On occasion, we could spy either the smoke or the masts of one of the blockaders, but none came close enough for us to risk a shot.

Of course I had the Enfield, which had a far greater range than the carbine. I kept it oiled and clean but still had scant ammunition for it, enough for three shots. Many in our company had surrendered their carbines for shotguns, but because of my demonstrated marksmanship, both on patrols and in practice, I was allowed to keep my Halls. We carried ourselves well in this patrol, even though we saw no action. After several days battling the wind and the steady attack of sea birds seeking to relieve us of our supplies, we shook the sand out of our blankets and headed back through the city.

Due to our constant drilling, we rode with great pride and precision, even in small groups. This gave an outward impression that we were the epitome of military decorum, even though I presume we presented a rather ragged sight at the end of our patrol. We found we had missed the ferry and would have to wait a while, so we rode around the city, accepting the admiring gaze of the citizens. Small gifts were bestowed upon us in the form of tobacco, bread, cakes, and pieces of hard candy. The privations of war were already starting to be felt and we knew it, so we would usually try to refuse these kindnesses but the gift-givers would have none of it. Several of us drew the attention of local girls, who would giggle at us then disappear behind a doorway or a hedge, then reappear to giggle anew. Having suffered the deprivations of camp life for so many months, we much appreciated this special attention.

As the hour of our departure came near, we were heading back to the ferry landing, and I heard a familiar voice call out to me.

"Jack!"

I turned and saw the visage of my father, ashen faced and worn far beyond his years.

"Jack! My boy! I was afraid you were dead and gone like your mother!"

I dismounted and approached him.

"Pa?"

"Yes, Jack, it's me!" He reached out to me but I instinctively pulled back.

He realized how I felt and just stood there smiling at me.

"I don't blame you, son, don't blame you one danged bit. But I've changed. I promise you. I'm working and don't drink nary a drop anymore. It almost killed me knowing you left. But then I realized it wasn't your fault at all, boy, it was me all along. I so regret the hardship I put on you. Can you find it in your heart to forgive me?"

I had already lived almost a full lifetime since I had run off, but this here was my pa, and tears formed in both of my eyes.

"Oh, Pa!" I said and we grasped each other's hands. "I'm sorry I left, but I was afraid of you."

"I know, son. I was a nasty, drunken muggins. I know it. But I've changed. I've let Jesus back into my life now, and He's rewarded me by bringing you back." He looked me up and down. "And look at you! You're a soldier?"

"Cavalryman," I said. "DeBray's Twenty-Sixth."

"Have you seen any action?"

"Patrols, mostly. Shot at some blockaders once."

He seemed impressed. "You're so young to be serving. Still I guess there's many a boy who's been called to grow up fast to serve their country."

"Jack?" It was the corporal. I guess he had been a witness to this reunion. "We best be going. The ferry will be landing soon. Excuse the interruption, sir."

"Pa, I need to go. We're camped near Houston. You can come out, mention my name. I... I'm in Company K."

"I will, son... Jack..." his eyes began to well up with tears, "it is just so good to see you... to know you are alive and well. I'm sorry for everything I've done."

I put my hand on his shoulder. "I'm doing really well, Pa, and I'm happy you've put your demons behind you."

"Behind me and long gone, I promise," he said.

I remounted Elvira, tipped my cap to Pa, and said, "Good to see you, but I've got to get going."

"I know, son. Godspeed," he said. "I live over in the Widow Hennessey's boarding house, you remember it?"

I said, "Yes," as I turned Elvira to follow the others. He waved as we rode off.

I looked back after we had gone about a hundred yards, and he was still there, one hand raised and waving as he watched me go.

"You ain't talked much about your pa." It was Robert Singleton from my squad.

"No," I said, "we had us some bad blood a while back. He drank too much, and then he'd get ornery and, well, I, uh, just, I just couldn't take it anymore. I was afraid he'd kill me."

"Maybe that's better now," he said. "He seemed genuinely glad to see you."

"We'll see," I said. "Not much chance of a grand reunion now, with this war going on."

After we boarded the ferry, the bay was choppy and a couple of the lads got sick. I had too much on my mind to think about getting sick.

I wasn't sure what I thought about seeing Pa again. Resentment ran deep, but then I thought more on it. He was my pa, and deep down, I knew I didn't resent him as much as I resented his drinking. As I studied on these thoughts, I whispered to myself as the ferry pulled in.

"Only time will tell."

Thirteen

In the fall of 1862, our patrols were increased because the blockading fleet began showing more activity. Ships frequently ran in close to the shore, causing much alarm among the populace. My squad visited Galveston several more times, and I managed to visit Pa on most of them. One day he even rode to the west end of the island and found us, bringing along a small quantity of coffee he had hoarded. This was a treat for us because we hadn't seen any in months.

Pa was quite vocal in his worries of the Federal presence.

"I am afraid Galveston will be invaded. The Yankees would love to deprive us of one of our major ports."

"Not if we can help it," we all chorused in return.

Patrol duty was boring. Except for that one brief action further down the coast, my patrols had not engaged any more Federals. We did see them from time to time if they ran in closer to shore, usually no closer than a mile or so. When they did this, we'd ride to the shoreline in force and we imagined to ourselves the sight of us made them veer away.

Back at camp, we would entertain ourselves as best as we could. Although food was getting scarce, for once we had clothing and shoes come in from the government. Most of us had become expert tailors since we had to keep our shirts and pants in good order, so when anyone received new trousers, they would immediately set to work reinforcing the seat since cavalry work was very hard on that area. We were hard on our shoes as well because we were often out in all sorts of weather.

By this time, Colonel DeBray began doing administrative work and Lieutenant-Colonel Myers was in day-to-day charge of the Twenty-sixth. He was a good and fair man, and we knew he had been hand-picked by the colonel to lead us. Every new patrol provided more reports of ships coming in close to shore. It was obvious to us there was some plan behind these actions.

On October 4, 1862, our worst fears were realized.

Robert White ran up to me with the news. "Federal gunboats entered Galveston harbor and demanded the city's surrender!"

Colonel Cook, the leading Confederate officer in the city, tried to negotiate but, faced with the destruction of the city by naval guns, he had no choice but to parley sufficient time to evacuate as many women and children as he could from the city.

Almost our full force was sent to the area of Virginia Point to aid in the evacuation. One trainload came to the mainland over the causeway with people and military supplies, but it was determined we did not want to let it fall into Federal hands so it never returned. Boats of all shapes and sizes sought to bring people to the mainland. I looked in vain but did not see Pa among them. Our company was busy helping maintain order amidst the chaos.

There was much consternation among the citizenry about the army's lack of action to prevent the Federal seizure of Galveston. I agreed with them. The Twenty-sixth, I thought, was one of the best units in the state, yet here we were, standing guard over the refugees. Galveston was an island, so in truth, there wasn't much we could do.

Our officers explained to us in more practical terms. "Cavalry is not much use against naval mortars and artillery."

Ship mounted guns were more massive than those utilized from shore. The only way to get to the island was by railroad or boat, so it was impossible for us to take up the fight. It made sense, but we were still incensed at our helplessness. The Union force deployed at Galveston was thought to be minimal, and our presence did little to dissuade these interlopers from carrying out their plan.

Sometimes a citizen would accost me in anger. "You there, soldier! Why aren't you doing anything to push those Yankees back into the sea? You're just prancing around on your horse."

I thought back and remembered a trick Moze had taught me.

"Talk calmly, don't let your anger take hold. It is the main way we slaves survive," he said. "Most of the time it works, too."

I would listen intently and calmly respond with something like, "Sorry, sir, I share your frustration, but I am just a soldier following orders. I can't stop an invasion alone, and besides, Galveston is an island, and cavalry can't go up against a Union gunboat."

Shortly thereafter, a flamboyant new commander for the sub-district of Texas arrived, General John Bankhead Magruder. He spared no time in reviewing the troops and assessing the situations. The Twenty-sixth was sent to Virginia Point to secure the tiny hamlet that overlooked the causeway containing the railroad bridge.

We were there to guard the docks and coast from any further Federal penetration. Rifle pits overlooked the causeway from both sides. We could hear the Federal ships in the harbor, blowing their whistles and mocking us from across the water. We did not detect much activity at the other end of the bridge, however, and by night we sometimes enlisted small boats to make the crossing and scout the immediate area of the bridge. Small patrols of Yankees were sometimes observed, but their occupation of the island was primarily concerned with harbor, docks, and wharves.

"What are we waiting for?" Rufus lamented to me one night.

"I reckon someone will come up with a plan before too long," I responded.

I was right. General Magruder decided to waste no more time and put forth a scheme to retake the island at our earliest convenience.

"They're going to plank the railroad bridge," Sergeant Murphy told us.

This meant stout lumber would be carefully laid across the tracks for its entire length. Although this would render it useless for locomotives, it would allow for the movement of troops and even horses across the bridge. For our part, once the planking was complete, we would establish a small post at the other end of the causeway to observe the enemy and send patrols to gather more intelligence.

The planking was done at night, employing the work of dozens of slaves impressed from neighboring farms and plantations. They were told to work silently lest they be tossed off the bridge. It was hard to see the work in the dark for they had chosen the darkest of nights to complete the task. Lumber was brought to Virginia Point by rail and then was ferried to the causeway by wagon in stages. Soon one could simply walk the length of the bridge from the mainland to the island.

After the planking was completed, a detachment from the Twenty-sixth was sent across with shovels and riflemen. I was one of the first to walk the narrow span.

Robert White kept me moving ahead of him. "Keep going, Jack, don't look down."

It was an eerie feeling walking against the ever-present coastal wind while I hovered unprotected just above the waters of the bay. The first time was the worst, but subsequent crossings got a bit easier. Nonetheless, my heart always beat about twice as fast as normal until I was safely on dry land again.

We took turns digging and guarding, lest any of us get too fatigued by the hard work. As soon as these fortifications were complete, we put our shovels aside and manned our posts. Signal lanterns flashed back and forth to allow communication, but they were simple as none of us knew the telegraph signals; we had prearranged simple flashes to signal the completion of the duty. Soon we were relieved from our posts, and I for one was glad. Guarding this post meant constant nervousness because we were expecting a Yankee counterattack at any moment.

The rumors started quickly. We were told someone would be dispatched on foot to scout the town. It was hoped we might learn of troop placement and movement. I must admit I was surprised when Captain Hare chose me for this duty.

"Jack, I have a dangerous mission for you but it is important."

"Just tell me what you need me to do, Captain."

"You're familiar with Galveston; is that correct?"

"I grew up there, sir."

"We need someone to go across the bridge, make their way into town, and find out what they can. It will be a great help to us."

"I'll do my best, sir."

"Although most people evacuated, we know some people remained."

"I think my father might be one of those. I haven't had any word from him since the Yankees arrived."

"If he's still there, it could be just the thing we need."

"I'll try to get up with him and see if he can help."

It was a week before Christmas when I went across the first time. I knew it was a dangerous mission, but I also knew the city very well, or at least I had known it. I was instructed to wear dark clothes but I had none. They did not want me in uniform lest I alert the Yankees to our intentions. In truth, I think the officers took advantage of my youth. I did not know then, but if I was caught out of uniform, they'd likely declare me a spy and I would most likely be shot. I borrowed a dark shirt and trousers from someone in another company.

It was a very dark night, and I followed a patrol across the bridge and rested in one of the rifle pits. Then I slowly made my way by following the railroad tracks a mile or so until I found a path we used to take when I was a child. It was little more than a cow path, but we used it to go down to the water to watch the workmen when they were building the causeway. It was great fun watching them and listening to them curse, and we would laugh when they slipped and fell into the water. Such an event would delight us because it would only make them scream and curse even more.

My heart was pounding as I made my way up this path, slowly and surely. Suddenly a black figure was blocking my progress. I heard,

"Shhh," and felt a hand grab my shoulder and pull me in close so I could see his face. It was Samuel, a boy I used to play with along the docks. Like me, Samuel had grown quite a bit since those days.

"Samuel?" I whispered.

"Yes, it's me, and now you're called *Captain* Jack?"

I blinked my eyes in disbelief. "What do you mean?"

"I knowed you was coming, so I high-tailed it out here to help guide you."

"How'd you know I was coming?"

"Da boo-hag done tolded me in a dream. Grabbed onto me like a bobcat onto a chicken, and I gots a picture in my head from her and I knowed it was you. She warnded me to meet you so here I is."

"I know the way," I said.

"Sure you do, but you don't know where them Yankees be hiding and I do. You wants your daddy, don't you?"

"Is he still here?"

"Yes, and I knows where he stays, so you just needs to follow me."

I crouched behind Samuel, and we made our way along the path into the town.

When we reached an area with more buildings, I was surprised at how eerie and deserted the town seemed. I expected a ghost or a Yankee to pop out at almost any moment. I had lived in Galveston all of my life, but I struggled to remember where I was and where I wanted to go. Samuel seemed to anticipate my wishes.

"Shhh. Soldiers."

I saw them and assumed they would be the Marines I was told I could expect to encounter. We stayed back in the shadows to avoid them.

I whispered, "I think he's at the widow Hennessey's."

"I knows where that is." Samuel pointed down a side street and motioned at me to follow him.

Finally I recognized a landmark as I walked behind him, and we quietly traveled the two blocks to the boarding house. As I approached it, Samuel stopped and put a finger to his lips. He pushed me on in front of him.

"I think you're good right here, but I'll be close-by if you needs me."

I patted him on the shoulder and moved on. I became aware of a figure on the porch and could vaguely see the features of his face from the glow of his pipe as he puffed. It was old man Schultz. He was a bit addle-brained, but I knew him to be an old friend of my Pa.

"Mr. Schultz," I whispered.

"Eh? Who's there?"

"Mr. Schultz, it's me, Jack Benson."

"Young Jack? Where'd you come from?"

"No matter. I need to see my pa, can you get him for me?"

I could just barely detect a wave of realization spread over the man's face as he seemed to remember something. "Oh, of course...yes, I'll get him. You best stay out of sight as there is a naval officer staying here. He's off one of those blasted blockaders."

He made his way inside the house, and I could hear the widow Hennessey fussing at him because he had not put out his pipe. I remembered that, although she allowed her tenants to smoke in their rooms, she did not allow such foolishness, as she called it, to be perpetrated in the common rooms. Things got quiet again for a few minutes before a new figure emerged.

"Jack?"

I was standing in the shadows on the far end of the porch. "Over here, Pa."

He shook my hand and clasped my shoulders.

"We shouldn't talk here," he said. "I know a quiet spot where we won't be disturbed. Follow me."

We went up an alleyway to a small alcove behind a store.

We both watched and waited for a minute to make sure we had not been followed.

"How in heaven's name did you get here?"

"Over the causeway. They sent me over to find out what is happening in town."

"My Lord, son, this is dangerous business. I had heard the bridge had been covered and a few troops were on the island, but I hoped it wasn't you."

"I know, Pa, but I have my duty to do."

"The Yankees are mostly camped out at the wharves," he said, "where a number of them have taken up residence. We've heard they were thinking about rousting your troops back off the island, but things have been quiet so they just sit tight. I believe they are waiting for additional soldiers."

"That's good to know. How are things here?"

"We are all cooperating because we don't want them to fire the town, but supplies are low. People were sneaking supplies over by boat for a while, but not much has come in lately. Mrs. Hennessey refused to evacuate. Said she wasn't leaving all her hard work to be pillaged by marauding Yankees. We have one naval officer who stays here several nights a week just to get off the boat, he says. She makes him pay her in gold pieces and he does."

"She don't miss a trick, does she?"

"No, the woman is as hard as nails."

"So can you tell me anything else about any troops?"

"Just some marines; they came in with the navy, best as I can tell. They keep their comings and goings fairly private. They patrol the harbor, and the ships come and go. They have brought in supplies but just barely enough for them, nothing for us. Like I said, rumors say they may bring more troops soon. We're lucky here because the widow had a pretty full larder, but she has a lot of mouths to feed."

"Okay, Pa. I appreciate you meeting me."

"You're my son, Jack. So are they coming in to save the town?"

"I'm just a private so I don't know much, but anything is possible."

I glanced around nervously because I had probably already told him too much. We heard footsteps off the alley, so we moved back farther into the shadows. It looked like two soldiers walking along.

"Night patrol," Pa whispered. The footsteps disappeared down the path.

"I am heading back, Pa, but you keep your eyes and ears open. They may send me here again."

"I will, son. And Jack?"

"Yes, Pa?"

"Be careful."

"I will, Pa. That's one reason they sent me along to see you. I know my way around and know how to avoid being seen. You never knew what sneaking around I did when I was a kid."

He stifled a laugh. "But to look at you, I'd think you were still a kid. What are you now? Sixteen?"

"Yes, as of October thirtieth."

He put his palm on my cheek. "I regret I was such a poor father to you in many of those years."

"It warn't you, Pa, it was the whiskey."

"Can't lay all the blame to the drink, boy. I have to shoulder the blame myself. That's one thing the preacher told me. It isn't the fault of the drink, it's the fault of the man. The only solace is we can choose to change our lives and I have. Losing you and admitting I was the reason you left was the key to me making the choice between changing my life and losing it."

"That's a powerful thought, Pa. I'm proud of you."

"I'm proud of *you*, boy. Now get out of here before you're discovered."

We shook hands and went our separate ways. I found my way back to the edge of town, then Samuel emerged from the darkness and pulled me down into some bushes.

"You'll wake the dead clomping around like that."

We waited a minute to make certain I wasn't followed, then we crept up the forgotten path back to the railroad line. When we got to the tracks, Samuel grasped both of my shoulders.

"Boo-hag told me you gonna lose this war to make us all free. Dat true?"

"I don't know what to make of it all. For me, it's about following orders."

"Sounds 'bout the same as living the slave life, don't it?"

I shrugged and said, "I imagine it's pretty close. But I need to get back."

"Well, I kept you safe, Captain Jack. Them's was *my* orders, I reckon."

"Thanks, Samuel. Stay safe."

"Ah knows my way back, Jack. *You* be safe."

I turned and followed the tracks until I knew I was getting close to the bridge and causeway. I made three short whistles, which was a prearranged signal. There was no answer. I made three more short whistles and finally heard the responding two which was the expected answer.

I crouched low and approached the position.

"Jack, is that you?" It was Tom Passmore.

I jumped over the edge of the pit and landed with a clump. "The whistle was supposed to tell you."

Tom shrugged. "Yeah, it was. Sorry Jack. What did you find out?"

"A little, not a lot, but I best go report to the captain."

We shook hands, and I crouched down and made my way across the long causeway where my information was passed on to the captain, who forwarded it to General Magruder himself.

Fourteen

I resumed my normal duties after reporting to the captain, and we all fell into a routine of watchful waiting. The Federals rarely ventured out of their stronghold with the exception of their gunboats, which moved freely between the harbor and their fleet offshore. Our outposts kept a faithful watch, but rumors ran rampant on our side.

"They are evacuating Houston."

"Jeff Davis has ordered an assault."

"General Lee is coming this way."

"We don't need General Lee, we have General Magruder."

There were rumors about our general as well. I heard, "He fell out of favor with General Lee during the previous summer's actions on the Virginia Peninsula, and as a result, President Davis sent him down to Texas to get rid of him."

I had drawn some courier duty, which meant I delivered communications between Virginia Point and Houston. As I fulfilled this task, I noticed some strange work being done along the Buffalo Bayou. Bales of cotton were being stacked on the decks of two boats, the *Bayou City* and the *Neptune*. They weren't being stacked like cargo; they were being made to look more like floating fortresses.

On one of my trips into Houston just before Christmas, the widow Jenkins saw me riding down the street and cried out to me.

"Jack! Jack! Is it really you?"

When I recognized her, I smiled and dismounted. I had not seen her in almost a year, and she reached out and drew me into the tightest hug I had felt in a long time.

"My word, Jack, I think you've grown! You are quite the soldier. And look at Elvira! You have taken good care of her, I see."

"Yes, ma'am. I'm just in town to exchange some correspondence."

"I can't get over the sight of you. You are quite the man now. It is hard to believe it has been almost a year since you went off and enlisted." She lowered her eyes and added, "Right after old Moze passed away."

"Yes, ma'am." I felt blood rush into my face; I was always shy when being fawned over. "How are you?"

"Oh, I'm fine. There are shortages of everything, but somehow we all manage to get by. I wonder...Jack, Christmas is in a few days. Would you like to come to the house for Christmas dinner? You could perhaps even bring one or two others. I would be proud to share my holiday meal in the company of some of our brave soldiers."

I happened to know Rufus, Robert White, and I were going to be available. All three of us were off the duty roster and we were already planning to spend our leave in Houston to perhaps find a hot meal and celebrate.

"I do have a leave," I said, "and was planning with two friends to come here anyway, but we had no set plans."

"Then you should all come to my house," she said. "There isn't much, but it will be hot and it will be good."

The widow Jenkins always seemed to make a good meal out of just about nothing.

"I can't speak for the other lads, but I will be here for sure. But, truthfully, I don't rightly expect they would ever turn down the chance for a home cooked meal."

"Can you be here by one o'clock?"

"Yes'm, unless the Yankees try to invade Houston or something. I will try to get word to you if something like that happens."

"Surely they wouldn't do anything on Christmas, would they?"

"I don't rightly know, ma'am. The Yankees seem to defy logic sometimes."

"Well, I hope to see you at one in the afternoon with your friends."

"Yes'm, it will be a true pleasure."

I remounted Elvira and continued on my way. I hoped I had not overstepped myself by including Rufus and Robert in the plans, but in truth, we had all lamented of late the fact that we missed some of the little comforts of home, what with the holiday approaching. When I returned to camp, I shared my news with Rufus and Robert.

"We have been invited to Mrs. Jenkins' house for Christmas dinner."

Rufus answered for both of them. "It's just about the best news I've heard since I joined up."

As luck would have it, we had just been issued new clothing from a recent procurement by the quartermaster. Unlike some of the others in the company, we chose to preserve our new outfits for this special Christmas dinner. On the appointed day, we finally availed ourselves of these crisp grey uniforms, fresh from the workshops in the Huntsville prison, and mounted our horses for the ride to Houston. We detected a wonderment of smells as we approached the door of Mrs. Jenkins' house.

"My, look at you fine soldiers," she said when she answered our knock.

"Ma'am, this here is Rufus Macomb and this is Robert White. Boys, this is the wi... uh, Mrs. Jenkins."

"Merry Christmas, boys. Please come on in and make yourselves at home."

Inside, she busied herself with completing the meal. The table was already set with some of her finest dishes. In my years living there with Moze, I had only seen her use those dishes three other times when she was entertaining some ladies from her church.

"I'm sorry, but when my slave Old Moze died, well, he almost always went out and shot the biggest wild turkey he could find for me. So many things are in short supply these days, but I managed to find two plump chickens to roast so we will be eating well. I also found a few potatoes and enough flour for hot biscuits, and there is still corn relish I put up last summer. And of course, those chickens have been stuffed. I hope you are hungry."

"We're soldiers. We are always hungry," we all said in unison.

The meal was everything we expected and more, and we spent a very pleasant afternoon with Mrs. Jenkins. We returned her hospitality by splitting enough wood for the entire season.

After we left, Rufus joked, "It's a wonder our horses can still carry us. Think of the extra weight we must be packing after eating so much."

That night, I was startled in my sleep. "It must be indigestion," I thought at first, and then my chest began to feel like someone had dropped an anvil on it, pushing down hard so I couldn't breathe. I couldn't see anything in the dark but knew my tent mates were sleeping soundly because I could hear them snoring. I broke into a cold sweat, and after long minutes of struggle, the feeling passed when my lungs suddenly filled with air. I had one overbearing thought rattling around in my head:

"Danger lies ahead of you. Take care, Captain Jack!"

In the morning, I could feel it before I saw it; the VV mark had returned to my shoulder. I spent a goodly amount of time clutching my trick bag and wondering to myself what Vanita had seen and what she meant.

~ * ~

When I woke up the morning of the thirty-first, I realized I had forgotten the anniversary of my enlistment, but in this moment, I took great pride in the fact that I had survived a year and three days in the service of our country. As I ate my breakfast of cold cornmeal, I received more news. It seemed General Magruder had planned something special to help celebrate my anniversary.

Sergeant Murphy came up and told us, "We are going to wrest Galveston from the hands of the Yankees."

Hundreds of infantry had been brought to Virginia Point, and for the first time, many of us caught sight of the resplendent figure of General Magruder, who was personally organizing the effort. Numerous troops and several pieces of artillery had been gathered. Companies B and E of DeBray's regiment were to go across the planked bridge and set up just outside the town on the bay side. The battle was to begin in the early morning hours. Company K would man the rifle pits on both ends of the causeway, ready to cover any retreat and counterattack.

The colonel spoke in his unique French-accented English. "Private, we want you to sneak back into the city. Do you think you can make contact with your father again?"

"I can try, sir."

"This will be dangerous. They will no doubt be aware of some of our movements, and they will be especially vigilant. You should wear your uniform, because if you are found prowling about in civilian clothes, you most likely would be shot as a spy."

I gulped. Deep inside, I had known that truth the first time, but it had never been thrust in my face in this way. "Yes, sir," I said.

I left Elvira in the care of Robert and informed him of my mission. "I wish I could tag along with you," he said.

I shook my head. "No, this is dangerous enough for one person. Two would make us more visible."

"Take care, Jack," he said.

"I will." We shook hands and then we parted company.

I made my way across the bridge and settled down in one of the rifle pits. Everyone in the company had known about my previous trip. I didn't know the fellows on duty this night but established the same whistle signal with them and made my way down the tracks. I found my old secret path and made my way to the city. I wondered if Samuel might join me, but this time, but he never showed. It didn't matter, I remembered the way flawlessly and got to the Hennessey house with no trouble. The house was dark. It was a cold night, and although I had been warm enough while moving, I began to catch a chill as I crouched, waiting for chance to get word to Pa.

As I waited, I was suddenly accosted from behind.

"What are you doing slinking around out here?" The voice was hard and officious. He held me close and gleaned a little of my features. "Wha...? You're just a boy."

It was a soldier. He called out to a comrade, and now I could hear the New England in his voice, remembered from my days prowling the docks.

"Fred, look what I found here. A prowler of some sort."

His associate approached and bellowed, "No one's supposed to be out here, boy."

"Just trying to see my pa," I said.

The loud voices had roused the house, and several occupants emerged, including Pa and the widow Hennessey, who was carrying a lantern.

"Go back in the house. No one is allowed to be on the street after dark."

"That's my boy," Pa said, "unhand him."

"Doesn't matter. Everyone should know the rules by now."

Just then, the widow Hennessey raised her lantern which unfortunately revealed the grey of my uniform.

"Ah-ha," said the first soldier, "A rebel!"

"Unhand him," Pa repeated.

"He's a spy!"

"He's no spy, he's in uniform. I fought in the Mexican War. A man cannot be considered a spy if he is in uniform. He's just here to see this gentleman, his father." It was old man Schultz.

I took the lead, "It's... It's true. I just sneaked away from my unit, back at the bridge. I miss my pa and wanted to see him, wish him a Happy New Year."

"Humph," said the soldier. "At best you're a deserter. In our army, deserters are shot."

The second soldier spoke up. "All this hubbub doesn't matter. If he's in uniform, he's a prisoner plain and simple."

Mrs. Hennessey countered. "But he's just a young boy."

"Go back into your house, ma'am. Here, boy, we're taking you in to our commander."

Any remaining protestations were squelched as I was promptly marched down the street. I cast one long look back at Pa, who was being held by Mr. Schultz.

"It's no use, Pa. I'll be okay. I promise." I could see tears welling in his eyes.

I recognized where they were taking me because I knew this part of the city better than any other. We arrived at the wharves where I was presented to the commander. He was the first Yankee officer I had ever seen in uniform, and he presented himself to me with a staunch military bearing, much like Colonel DeBray.

"What's this, Private?"

"Prisoner, Captain. We caught him prowling around over by the big boarding house."

The captain held a lantern close. "Why, he's just a boy. What are they doing over there, conscripting schoolboys?"

"He says he was just trying to visit his father, sir."

"Is that true, boy?"

"Yes, sir. Stationed across the way. I just wanted to make sure my pa was okay."

"Do you know you could be shot as a spy?"

"How could I be a spy, sir? I'm in uniform." I was glad Mr. Schultz had given me this idea.

The captain smiled. "Well, right you are. What can you tell me about the sound of movement we hear? There's always something going on around that bridge, but tonight there seems to be more of it."

"I'm just a private, sir. I don't rightly know."

"What unit are you with?"

"Cavalry, sir."

"What unit?"

I didn't answer.

"Well, then what's your name, your rank?"

"John Benson, sir, private."

"Well, Private Benson, you are a prisoner of war now." He looked up to one of the other soldiers and said, "Private, put Benson here in chains and escort him to the dock. The bark *Louisa* is about to set sail for the fleet to deliver correspondence. He is to be transferred to one of the blockaders for transport. We have no facility for prisoners here; let the navy have him for a while to keep him out of harm's way."

"Yes, sir," came the reply, and once I was shackled, off we marched.

My heart was racing so hard I thought it would break right out of my chest and splatter my shirt with blood. I had known the risks, and now, it seemed I was about to pay for my failure. I would have given anything to be back in the saddle on Elvira, alongside Rufus and Robert, waiting to mount the attack. I lurched forward as the guard shoved me along. Yes, I was scared, but in the back of my mind, I kept reminding myself I was a soldier. One thing the army life had taught me was to take each new challenge and meet it as best as I could.

I thought back and remembered something Moze had once said, *"If you can't change something, just wait a while and maybe something else will come around the corner that will change it for you."*

I was comforted by this thought as we arrived at the dock. I knew enough of shipboard routines to see the boat was making swift preparations to cast off.

"Hold! I have additional cargo for you...a prisoner to transport to the fleet."

A naval officer was standing at the gangplank. "A prisoner? We have no facility to transport a prisoner."

"Captain Grainger's orders, sir. He was just captured in town."

The officer sighed. "All right, all right, bring him aboard." He drew a sidearm and pointed it at me. "No trouble out of you or you'll be a dead prisoner."

"No trouble, sir," I said, jangling my shackles as proof.

As soon as I was aboard, I heard him say, "Cast off!"

The ship eased away from the dock, and we began to move out into the harbor. The other vessels we passed were quite impressive, some of them sporting several pieces of artillery. We quietly steamed past them and headed in the direction of the Gulf of Mexico. Just as we made our way around Bolivar Point, we heard the booming sound of artillery behind us, a lot of it, and I knew the attack had begun.

Fifteen

With the cannon fire thundering in the background and no understanding of what was going on, the naval officer had me further secured with ropes to a mast-like structure on the deck. The movement across the water and the spray from hitting waves greatly enhanced the chilly January night, and I shivered as I sat on the deck. We continued to hear muffled sounds of battle behind us. The officer draped a blanket around my shoulders and crouched down to where I was sitting.

"What would that be?" he asked. "Your friends attacking the town?"

"I wouldn't know. I crossed into Galveston to see my father. He lives there."

"Most likely everyone will be killed in the battle. We don't let ports we capture fall back into enemy hands," he said.

I looked down. "I just pray my pa is safe."

"No matter, secesh," he said. "From what they told me, you were captured across the lines in uniform, so you will be treated as a prisoner of war."

It was the first time I'd heard the word directed at me and I didn't like it. Secesh was a derogatory term used by some Yankees to show their disdain for southerners who had dared to secede from the union.

He brought a lantern closer and examined my face. "Why, you're just a boy. How did you ever get into the army?"

"The cavalry," I said. "I know my way around horses, and I am the best rifleman in my company, that's how."

"Oh, I see," he said with a laugh. "Well, we'll make sure you are out of the war, for a while anyway." He walked away, still looking aft toward the diminishing sounds of fighting behind us.

The thundering booms faded as we proceeded further toward the dark horizon. I had no way of knowing if General Magruder's plan had worked or if my father was safe. Before long I noticed a flurry of light signals and various other activities around me on the deck. I struggled for a moment before I could stand. I could see some lanterns on a much larger ship not too far away. We soon pulled alongside and ropes were thrown. There was a mild roll on the ocean, but it was a fairly calm night.

The officer stood at the side of our ship. "You, there. Secesh. Come here."

A sailor untied the ropes binding me to the mast and I walked over to him.

The officer called up to the other boat. "We have a prisoner to transfer."

"Prisoner? From where?"

"Galveston. I don't know anything about him. There were rumors of a coming action before we left port. We heard artillery as we rounded the point. He may have been an advance guard or picket or something. He was transferred to us just as we were leaving."

"We heard the cannon fire as well. All right, bring him aboard. We'll take him to New Orleans with us and let them deal with him."

I was hoisted to the other ship like a piece of cargo and sent below to the boiler room where I was told to sit against a wall opposite the boilers. A couple of Negroes were hard at work stoking the fires. I assumed the ship was going to steam away after everything was secured.

The officer told them, "This man is a prisoner of war, don't let him leave."

I was regarded with wide eyes but their work continued. I didn't mind this scrutiny much because at least it was warm down there.

Soon, the familiar sounds of the steam engine filled the ship, and with a groaning lurch, we began to move. Despite the cold, I preferred the deck so I could see what was going on. Watching these men shovel coal with monotonous frequency allowed fatigue to overtake me and I soon drifted off to sleep.

I was awakened some time later by a gentle shake.

"Hey, boy, you want some grub?"

It was one of the two stokers, crouching beside me.

"We'ze got some food, you hongry?"

In truth I was famished. "Yes."

He thrust a hard cracker into my hands and placed a small tin cup of water next to me. The other stoker joined him.

"Why, you'ze just a boy," he said. "I'ze Malachi. Dat dere is Custus."

"Jack," I said before I tried to nibble a corner of the cracker. It was so hard it hurt my teeth.

"Where they grab you?"

"Galveston City," I said.

"Wuz you fighting? We heard tell of some distant booms, cannon probably."

"I think there was fighting but I wasn't in it. I sneaked into town to see my pa."

"And they grabbed you? Good thing you wuz in uniform or they'd a shot you sure 'nuff. Dip that hardtack in the water to soften it up some."

I did as he instructed, and it made it a little easier to break off pieces to chew on. It had little taste, but due to my hunger, I quickly devoured it.

"What ship is this?" I asked.

"This here's the *Hatteras*, bound for N'awlins."

I knew New Orleans was now a Federal outpost. Having seen little of the real war, we knew almost nothing of the handling of prisoners. I heard of prisoner paroles and exchanges, with the parolees being bound by honor not to return to the conflict. This was something most of them ignored...or at least it was the common belief. I assumed the Yankees did the same thing. I drifted off to sleep again, and before too long, I realized Malachi was stretched out beside me. There were two other men shoveling coal. I had no idea where Custus was.

Malachi noticed I had stirred. "Snatching me some sleep. I usually sleeps on deck, but it too cold tonight."

Soon he was snoring the night away.

At one point, Malachi began to have some distress and I woke up. He was gasping for breath in a pitiful hopeless sort of way. Both of the new stokers ran over to assist, but all everyone did was watch as he struggled. They seemed afraid.

"Hag-ridden!" I heard one of them say.

"Boo-hag, my mama calls it."

"That's the dang South Carolina in you, boy," the first joked.

Finally, when he seemed more settled, I reached out with my bound hands and shook him. He was trembling and drenched in sweat but opened his eyes and managed a huge intake of air, like his lungs had been constricted by some heavy weight that had been suddenly lifted. He began blowing in short wheezes until he managed to catch his breath and calm down.

"Hag got me good," he gasped. "Some witchin' spirit clomped down on my chest. I couldn't breathe."

A seaman came by to see what the problem was.

"You two, get back to work before we lose steam."

"Yessir, boss."

They went back to the coal pile as he crouched down, "What's the problem here?"

"I'm afeared it was some hoodoo mischief, I couldn't breathe none."

I immediately thought of Vanita, but I said nothing.

"Nonsense. You strained a muscle shoveling and had a cramp, that's all. Go on, now, get your rest." He looked over at me. "Keep an eye on him."

When the seaman was gone, Malachi leaned over and whispered, "You said your name was Jack. Is you *Captain* Jack?"

I was wide eyed this time. "In the army, I'm just Jack," I said. "Where did you hear...?"

"The hag. She whispered in my ear after she got my attention. Said she was a trick-doctor called Vanita and you wuz Captain Jack and I wuz to keep you safe."

Malachi was shirtless, and I saw the dark outline of VV forming on his shoulder. I must have turned a shade of grey.

"You okay, boss?" Malachi was gently shaking me.

"Yes," I said, but my mind was racing and I was in shock.

Many thoughts ran through my head in quick succession. "Vanita? Here, miles at sea?" What deviltry was this? I was afraid.

Then I remembered Moze's dying wish was my safety in war, and I also thought back to the night on the boat. Vanita had assured me I was safe when she was with me. The previous incidents had been closer to home, so I had always half-thought perhaps she had gotten word somehow to other slaves. I had kept the notion of magic at arms-length, respectful, but not really believing in it. But now it seemed all too real. I struggled a bit until I worked the small trick-bag out of my trouser pocket, raised it to my lips and kissed it, then held it out in the light. I had never even opened it, but I had always respected it and 'recharged it' in the full moon as she had instructed.

Malachi's eyes got wide again when he caught a glimpse of it. "Trick bag!" he whispered. "She give it to you?"

I nodded.

"Put it away, please. I'll watch out for you while you're here. I will. I promise. I don't want no hoodoo curses following me the rest of my born days."

I put it away.

The next two days were a blur of boredom except when I was taken out on deck. Out there I observed an array of artillery and sailors. Both days I was given coffee, which I relished. Our supplies had gradually diminished, so it was a pleasant surprise to see it lavished on a prisoner so far out to sea. I held the cup of precious liquid in my hands and blew on it before I sipped, then gulped the contents.

Malachi had apparently spread the word, because after that night every Negro on the boat treated me with an abiding respect. These men bequeathed me with extra rations and even some sweets. I was never in want of a blanket or an extra cup of soup. This attention confused the white sailors since I was, after all, one of the accursed rebels.

After we docked in New Orleans, I became something of a puzzle to the authorities. No one really knew what to make of me. I was in uniform, but there were no papers explaining exactly how I came to be a prisoner. I figured it was Yankee business, so I kept my mouth shut. My apparent youth confounded them, and I stuck with the same story: I was just visiting my father.

I heard one officer say, "Why are we even bothering with this boy? The story is all hearsay and circumstantial."

I wasn't sure what he meant, but I knew the implication could go both ways: harsh treatment as a prisoner or release because they weren't sure they had a right to hold me. For the most part, I don't think the New Orleans commander wanted any part of the responsibility, so he endeavored to pass me down the line to some other authority. Since the navy had brought me in, I was remanded back to the navy once again.

All they knew about me was my name, rank, and the fact I had been captured as a prisoner of war in Galveston. I was transferred to another steamer bound for New York City with captured cotton and other supplies along with a lot of official correspondence. We set sail the next day.

Our trip suffered a spate of bad weather, and the steamer struggled in the face of at least one bad Nor'easter, the sailors called it, and I spent most of it sick as a dog. For me, the entire voyage was a blur of cold, cramps, and misery. The one solace was in the gentle treatment

I received from the several Negroes on board. It seems my fame had spread, probably thanks to Malachi. I was surprised to see the Federal navy made such wide use of freedmen, but I was glad of it.

Every day, I received refreshing whispered encouragement to "Captain Jack" when they brought me bits of hardtack, jerky, water, soup, and cups of that luxurious coffee. For the life of me, I had no recollection of any real reason I might deserve such fame. Quite the contrary, I was a soldier from a country endorsing the enslavement of their race, despite my own feelings on the matter. Still, in spite of these kindnesses, the overall misery of the trip was almost unbearable.

It was a definite relief when we finally docked in New York City. I was taken to an old fortification out in the harbor bordering a place I had previously heard of called Brooklyn. Fort Lafayette was my new home for the time being, although the nature of my captivity was still a mystery to everyone.

Sixteen

There was not much to the prison. The place was an old fort in the harbor, about a quarter of a mile from the shore. I imagine it was built to defend New York from invasion, but since the Yankees had no fear of Jeff Davis invading the grandest city of the Union, they thought it would make a dandy prison. I suppose it did. Some prisoners seemed to be Yankees who in some manner, shape, or form opposed the war and the policies of President Lincoln.

"It is unconstitutional to hold us here," many of them said.

Some such term as *habeas corpus* was bandied about quite a bit along with a lot of grumbling that Lincoln had suspended the use of it. Whatever it meant, it apparently allowed him to put anyone he didn't like in jail. Anyway, I think this was their general feeling.

Other prisoners were captured from privateer blockade runners. This seemed to be how I ended up in this place, due to the fact that I had been entrusted to the care of the blockade fleet after my capture. But I seemed entirely out of place there in my military uniform.

In fact, my appearance accorded me a bit more respect from my military captors, but I think they considered most of these other souls with disdain. The privateers were held in chains most of the time. I think the guards could at least appreciate me as a military man, despite my youth.

There was one obvious difference in our care. For many of the prisoners, the food was not very good. However, they could procure better food if they had money or to be more precise, had been captured with some money, which had, of course, been confiscated. This was the case for most of the privateers and for the Yankee prisoners. I had no such means to augment my rations.

As I've said several times before, my captors did not know what to do with me. Lieutenant Wood, the officer in charge, was befuddled by my age, and since I had been accompanied by scant military records and had been given only one interview in New Orleans, there was a bit of confusion as to why I was sent to this place. Very early on in my incarceration, I decided it would be to my advantage to play along with this confusion.

One thing I had perceived was that Yankees were all prim and proper as pertains to the appearances of things. Officers in general were much inclined to keep a lot of papers, making sure every tiny detail was according to regulations and in order. I did not fit into their model of things. Without such details, I was a question mark to Lieutenant Wood, and I could tell early on he did not like things in such disarray.

I was interviewed a number of times after my arrival, and to my way of thinking, I figured that if he did not know enough details of my situation, I would not hasten his understanding.

A typical interview would go like this:

"Why are you here? You're just a boy."

"Cavalryman, sir." Colonel DeBray's training in military courtesy served me well in this, and I always felt my crisp demeanor impressed Lieutenant Wood.

"How did you come to be a prisoner of war?"

"Captured, sir."

"I know that, boy, but where?"

"There was a battle at Galveston, sir. I am a private in a cavalry unit, and I was captured and put on a boat as your navy exited the island."

I would repeat these same replies whenever asked. In one of these interviews, I learned Magruder's gamble had paid off and Galveston had been abandoned by the Federals; this was a good support to my mention of capture.

As new prisoners came in, he soon lost interest in me, so I endeavored to gain a bit of favor by making myself useful in many ways to my jailors. This was nothing new to how I regarded any situation, for Moze had instilled in me the notion that idle hands were not good. There was always something needing to be done. This cemented in my captors' minds the notion I was, after all, just a poor lost boy without a penny to his name.

In DeBray's battalion, I downplayed my youth. I was a soldier and a man in my mind, and in return, to all I encountered. Here, I very much played up the fact that I was just sixteen. I didn't care who knew this detail, and whenever possible, I took advantage of their softness to my situation.

Through this tactic and my willingness to work, I quickly gained the trust of my captors and earned a few extra rations and a bit more freedom of movement. A man by the name of Skylar, the ordnance sergeant who handled the arrangements for feeding the more affluent prisoners, worked with his wife in that regard, and she was always very nice to me when she arrived with these extra meals. Very early in my confinement, I also noticed she was sometimes accompanied by her daughter, who I occasionally caught watching me out of the corner of her eye.

On one of those days, I was sweeping a corridor, and this pretty young woman handed me a small packet wrapped in a handkerchief. When I unwrapped the pink ribbon tied around it, I saw a light blue P embroidered in the corner.

"I embroidered P on it for my name, Pearl," she said. Her smile was like the dawn of a sunny new day to me.

I opened the folds and found a small piece of cake. I looked back at her and smiled my obvious approval. It was a wonderful interlude in my otherwise dreary existence, for the food we were fed was quite awful.

"Thank you, Miss Pearl," I said. "My name is Jack Benson."

"I baked the cake myself," she said, almost blushing. Her blue eyes were framed by soft skin the color of cream when it has just topped in a jug of fresh milk. Her chestnut hair was streaked with honey colored strands that reflected light in a most amazing way. "My mother is better at general cooking, but I'm told I have quite a knack for baking. My grandmother taught me."

I forgot my manners and gobbled the cake in two bites because I was quite hungry.

"I'm sorry, but I'm famished. It's really good!" I wiped frosting off my chin and licked my fingers.

As she turned to follow her mother, I heard a slight giggle that made my heart flutter.

Every few days, she accompanied her mother, and she always brought me some new sweet confection she had created. I'd chat with her, slowly savoring the delightful flavor of whatever cake or cookie she had bequeathed to me as I leaned against the hard, cold stone walls.

One day, when the weather was mild, we ventured out to a small enclosed area where prisoners could spend some time outside. We were generally allowed out into this open area of the fort twice each day, but as I said, my extra duties afforded me some privileges. Her mother watched carefully from a window as we chatted. I don't know why Mrs. Skylar allowed us this luxury, but I much enjoyed basking in the glow of Pearl's delightful smile.

"Jack, forgive me if I am too forward, but could you answer a question for me?"

"Of course, Pearl."

"Why do you insist on fighting against us? I mean, it's cost you your freedom. Is it worth that much to you? Isn't what you do treason against your country?"

I took a deep breath. Many times since my captivity, I had pondered these same questions.

"I'd be the first to say I don't know much about the ways of governments, but I can say most of the people I know don't consider it to be treason. I've seen some of what is outside these walls," I said, waving at the enclosure. "The United States seems to be doing just fine without us. In Texas, the elected folks decided it was best for us to make our own way. Once they did that, well, to my way of thinking, it was up to the rest of us to follow along and protect the part we had left."

"So you think what you're doing is right and just? Even keeping slaves?"

I sighed heavily. "I'm not rightly sure about that part. I've lived my whole life thinking it was the normal state of things. Now, although I know it's the biggest part of the whole deal, I can't say I'm too much for it. But a man makes his decisions and needs to stick by them. I'm sure I'll never own nobody, but for now, I'm just a soldier trying as best as I can to do my duty as I see it. Once you're a soldier, you see, the bigger things get blurred. You are most concerned with your comrades, and you go to battle because *they* go to battle, not because you believe in one thing or another. We all, each and every one of us, depend on one another."

"But you're my age, Jack, you're just a boy, same as I'm just a girl."

"I reckon I've moved far beyond such a distinction in the last year or so."

"But surely you know keeping slaves is wrong."

I hung my head low for a moment then looked in her lovely eyes again. "When I was a child, I played with kids, slave and white, and to me we were all just the same as anybody. Now I judge people by what they do. Worst white man I ever knew was my pa. He drank and beat me every day until I just couldn't take it anymore and ran away. On the other hand, the best *friend* I ever had was a slave, Moze, who took me under his wing and taught me right from wrong and how to shoot and hunt. I was hired to watch over him, but in truth, he watched over me a hundred times over."

"So don't you want him to be free?"

"He's as free as he's ever going to be. He died right before I joined up."

She put a hand to my shoulder. "Oh, Jack, I'm so sorry."

"It's all right. He lived a long life. I guess it was his time."

"But did he like being a slave?"

"No, I know he didn't, but he was a master at making the best of his situation."

"My mother said you could likely recant your allegiance to the South and be released from prison."

"I don't reckon I can do that. I swore me an oath. I wouldn't be much of a man if I went against a solemn oath, would I? I haven't suffered the hardships of these last months to just give up. I owe a good deal of respect to my comrades. Pearl, understand, to me *that* would be treason."

She turned her head as her mother called from a doorway. "Pearl, we need to be getting back now."

"Jack, I want you to know something. I think you *are* a man. I may not agree with everything you say, but I surely admire the way you stand up for your principles. I want you to think about something else, too."

"What?"

She leaned forward and placed two of the softest things I've ever felt in my life on my cheek. I quickly glanced at her mother and couldn't tell if she was exhibiting a smile or a smirk, but I felt my face flush as if I had a fever.

The next day, Pearl came to see me again with another small piece of cake. We walked to a far section of the open compound, and I ate it quickly.

"My father fussed at my mother for allowing me to give you food without paying."

"I appreciate your kindness, and they have been delightful treats for me. I had no money when I was captured, so I can't afford the cost of his meals."

"I know. I still don't quite understand how such a young man came to be a soldier."

"I was big for my age and willing, I guess."

"How do you face the horror of battle? I've seen some men who have been crippled or terribly disfigured from wounds."

"In truth, I haven't seen much in the way of battle. I took a few shots at some Union navy men one time when we were on patrol, but I couldn't bring myself to aim at them. I'm a good shot, mind you, better than most, but I aimed at their water barrels and the sides of their boat. I guess I was more intent on scaring them off so I didn't have to fight them."

Pearl placed her soft hand on my cheek. "There may be some hope for you yet, Jack Benson."

Some days later, Mrs. Skylar approached me, accompanied by Pearl, who held a cloth bag.

"Here, Jack, I brought you something," she said.

"What is it?" I asked.

"Just look." Mrs. Skylar had spoken but Pearl was beaming.

I opened the bag and saw some folded civilian clothes. I pulled out a warm jacket, a very nice shirt, a pair of trousers, and two pairs of clean socks.

"Your uniform looks so ragged and dirty, I thought perhaps you'd like something newer and more comfortable." Mrs. Skylar exchanged a glance with Pearl, but both continued to smile at me.

I blinked back a couple of tears. I had been wearing my uniform for weeks, and I relished the thought of a change of clothes, even if it would just allow me time to wash it.

"Well, I, I... I just don't quite know what to say," I said.

"I so miss the sound of a soft Southern accent," she said, and added, "but you don't have to say anything. I have a neighbor lady in the city whose son was killed in Virginia, and she was glad someone could get some use out of them. I didn't mention I wanted them for a Southern soldier, though."

The thought of wearing a dead man's clothes gave me pause, but I lost any notion of impropriety when I felt the softness of the garments.

Pearl spoke up. "Now you go and change your clothes and give your uniform to me."

"I can't lose my uniform," I said, "at least not until after I'm paroled or exchanged."

"I know, silly. I'll wash it up nice and laundered for you." And she brought it back the next day, crisp and clean.

Several days later, her mother passed me in the hall.

"Jack, why aren't you wearing your new clothes?"

"I'm saving them. I want to get all the use I can out of my uniform before I ruin them. Where has Miss Pearl been? I've missed our chats."

"Pearl caught a chill and has been ill. I've sent her up the Hudson to stay with my mother. The cold, wet climate of this fort is the worst thing for her."

"I'm so sorry," I said. "Will she be all right?"

"We're hopeful, but she needs to recover. Jack, I know she is quite fond of you, and it is another reason I sent her away. She's a young girl and has silly notions she can sway you away from your duty. I'm the wife of a soldier, and I know that is almost impossible. I've let her chat with you because it made her happy, but her father and I think it is best for both of you to stop it now."

I lowered my chin to my chest. "I'm quite fond of her, too, but I know you are right. One day, I'll go back and probably never see her again." A tear rolled down my cheek.

"My husband is quite distressed I let these things go along the way they have. He is certain her hopeless infatuation has something to do with the decline in her health. I am fond of you, too, Jack...I'll try to sneak you a tidbit from time to time."

"Thank you for all of your kindnesses," I said.

"Oh, and Pearl wanted you to have this." She handed me something small. "Don't look at it until I'm gone, please, lest my husband see it."

I unfolded it when I was alone. It was a small cookie wrapped in one of her handkerchiefs, embroidered with the letter P.

~ * ~

After that encounter, my life settled back into the drudgery of confinement. We normally ate two meagre meals of awful food a day, along with coffee. I had become quite fond of coffee, even the miserable, watered down version they served us, and I knew I was going to miss it when I got back. It was only grown in far off places of the world and had to be brought in by ship. In Texas, the blockade took care of that small detail, although some small supplies of it made it across the border with Mexico.

I talked with the captured blockade runners sometimes and asked one if he ever brought coffee in as cargo.

"There's no money in coffee for us. It's valuable, but we can't carry it in sufficient quantities because what the South wants is guns and powder."

As a soldier, I guess I could understand, but I knew other fellows in my outfit missed it something awful. I sometimes thought on the subject, and I calculated that I could be a rich man if I could figure out a way to get coffee across the lines to our side. The privateers in chains told the other side of the story, though, so I let my fantasy slide away.

It being January when I arrived, I was colder than I had ever been in my life. The coat Pearl and her mother had given to me served me well in this regard. It was the only item of the civilian clothes I wore regularly. Of particular interest to me were the quantities of snow the sky dumped on our location.

It was a rarity where I lived in Texas, and I had seen snow only once in my life. The memory of this singular event still lingered, but here, one storm gave me my fill of the stuff. That snowstorm was followed by another and then several more. Because of my expressed willingness to help around the fort, I was asked to accompany some men shoveling the snow from the open area to facilitate the daily exercise periods. I will take digging a latrine trench any day over the back-breaking work of shoveling snow. I guess the digging was similar, but it was bitterly cold. The numbing pain in my feet and hands were the worst. Still, I got to extend my outside time a little, and the fresh air and physical exertion helped me to keep my spirits up.

Our confinement quarters were originally part of the gun batteries, and through the small openings in the outer wall, I could see various merchant ships and military vessels moving in and out of the harbor. The city adjacent to the island seemed almost endless from my limited vantage point. Seeing the boats reminded me of my youth along the wharves at Galveston, but this scene was many times multiplied.

I fell into a certain routine in the prison. As prisoners came and went, I continued to use my familiarity to get things like additional food and coffee. Mrs. Skylar gave me tidbits from time to time but never spoke of Pearl again, for Sergeant Skylar kept a watchful eye.

Newspapers were a common treat, and I usually scrambled for my share of a page. These were much in demand, and I think the guards gave them to us to watch us argue and fight over them. I was amazed to see just how much information those northerners had available to them.

Back in Texas, we heard bits and snatches of intelligence, and one didn't know what was real and what was rumor. Here, we were aware of a constant stream of what I assumed was real news.

I learned of the Union defeat at a place in Virginia called Fredericksburg. It had happened before my capture, but I didn't read about it until several weeks after I arrived. Then there were the stories about a general named Grant who was trying to box up a holdout city named Vicksburg that overlooked the Mississippi River. There was much speculation about the fate of the South if the city fell.

One day, I read about the sinking of the U.S.S. *Hatteras* by the infamous raider C.S.S. *Alabama*. Even though it was considered a Confederate victory, I did have a brief history with the *Hatteras*, and I worried for the fate of the stokers who had befriended me, especially Malachi and Custus. But fate works in strange ways sometimes. My situation would have been fatally changed if I had been aboard when it was attacked.

At times like this, I contemplated the power of my trick-bag. Although I had been searched when I arrived, it was not found, even though it was right there in my pocket. Every full moon, I did as Vanita had instructed and secreted the bundle under its gaze. There were no trees to hide it in, so I put it in the corner of one of the gun parapets. We were always made to snuff our candles at nine, so this was easy to do when it was pitch black. Yes, I was a prisoner, but I was surviving. I considered that to be good luck, so I felt compelled to respect the bag's power.

One day, I was helping stack some supplies being delivered from the mainland. Some free blacks were unloading the boat while several of us prisoners moved the cargo and stacked the crates in a storeroom. During the course of my labor, my trick bag worked its way out of my pocket and fell to the dock. The red flannel was quite obvious, and it attracted the attention of our guard, who had been stationed to supervise because those of us from the fort were all prisoners.

"Ho, prisoner, what's that bag?"

I reached down and picked it up and began to put it back in my pocket.

"I said, what is that bag? Give it to me."

As he reached out his hand, one of the Negroes intervened.

"You don'ts want none o' that, sir. Trick-bag. Magic."

"Posh."

I hesitated.

"I'm telling you the truth, you don'ts wants no part of it," and he turned and looked at me. "Ain't I right?"

"It's just for good luck," I said.

I handed it over, and the solder felt around the outside of it, then began to open it.

The Negro held his ground. "Ah wouldn't open it."

"What's in it?"

"Probably trinkets and herbs and such." He again looked at me. "Ain't it?"

"I suppose so. I've never opened it. An old witch woman back home gave it to me to protect me. Supposed to be good magic," I said.

"It's *hoodoo!*" the Negro said. "Might be good magic or bad magic." He pointed at me, "Wut's good for him," he said, turning his finger to the guard, "probably be bad for you."

The guard's face flushed as he felt the outside of the bag and began to hand it out to the Negro to hand back to me. "I guess it's all right."

"Don't be giving it to me. I don't wants to touch it," he said.

The guard reached out and gave it to me. "Just never saw it before. I suppose if you've had it all this time, it is all right."

I took the bag and stuffed it deep in my pocket.

~ * ~

One day, Lieutenant Wood asked me to accompany him to headquarters on shore. I supposed it was perhaps a reward for my helpful service. We boarded a small boat and soon approached what they called Brooklyn. I was quite shocked at the hustle and bustle of the city. There were more people scurrying about than I had ever seen in one place. I supposed at the time Brooklyn probably had more people than all of Texas. It was late February, and a chill wind swept through the streets as we hurried along. We approached a building with a guard.

"You will be seeing Major Lloyd, adjutant in charge of prisoners here in the New York vicinity," he said.

I was escorted into an ornate office where I was instructed to sit down.

"Private Benson, I have been reviewing your case. Your situation is quite unique. I commend you, sir, you have been a model prisoner. Are you just a well-mannered young man or does your army have such discipline?"

"My commander prides himself on our discipline, sir."

"I believe it," he said. "Now, as I was saying, your case is quite unique. You came to us under very odd circumstances, and I have pondered long and hard on what to do with you."

I bobbed my head slightly, still at attention.

"The way I see it, you have four options. You could remain a prisoner, of course. Normally, I would be inclined to offer you a chance to enlist in our own army, but sadly, it's not possible, given your age." He grinned at me. "We could use a man like you. Now, we could simply parole you and release you here. That is what I really want to do, but of course, you are young and alone and know no one in this city. It might be an unfair burden to you."

"And the fourth option?" I asked.

"We could send you down to City Point in Virginia to be exchanged along with other prisoners of war. You were obviously captured in uniform, even if the facts are not fully substantiated."

"Do I have a say in the matter?"

"Not fully, but I will entertain your comments."

"I am a soldier, sir, and I would prefer to be exchanged with other prisoners."

"I had a feeling this would be your choice. But understand, if you would consider the parole, I want you to know I have friends here and could perhaps help you to get situated. There are many opportunities here for a fine, polite, and industrious young man like yourself."

"You ever know anyone from Texas, sir?"

"Yes, I did some service at outposts in Texas in the old army before the war."

"If you have known some of us, you know we all feel like there is Texas in our blood. I need to get home."

He laughed after I said this and added, "In my experience, I know what you have just said is true enough. So you want to go to City Point?"

"Yes."

"So be it then. I will formally request you be transported to City Point for exchange. Son, I have only heard good things about you, but I want you to know something. Trust me, we will win this war. You would do a lot better for yourself to be on the winning side."

"I've watched the ships coming and going with supplies and…" I had tears welling in my eye, "I know what you say is true. But, sir, I have a duty to my country the same as you."

At this, the officer stood up and saluted me. I returned the salute and he shook my hand. "I can expect no more from a good soldier. Good luck to you, Private."

"Thank you, sir."

After several days, I was told to prepare my belongings, which was not hard since I had almost nothing to my name but my uniform and my few articles of civilian clothes. A guard accompanied me as a guide, and we departed from the fort. Once on the mainland, we quickly negotiated the alien landscape of Brooklyn. We eventually found ourselves at a dock bordered by a large vessel. I could see it was making preparations to embark, I assumed to Virginia.

Seventeen

I was told the ship would not depart for another two hours. The guard reached out and handed me a ten-dollar gold piece before he left.

"Here, the lieutenant wanted me to give you this."

I held the coin in my hand for a moment, shocked. "Give him my thanks."

I stood on the dock, unsure what to do. I assumed I was not under guard because I had no other place to go. I wondered to myself for a moment if perhaps I should take advantage of the situation and perhaps just find passage on a ship going to some foreign land. But I remembered Robert, Rufus, and my other comrades back in Texas, and I knew I needed to get back for their sakes. I pushed the notion of escape out of my mind.

Because I had a little time before the departure, I thought I might explore the surrounding area a little. Before leaving the fort, the guard suggested I change to my civilian clothes to walk the streets of Brooklyn.

"You Johnny Rebs have killed many a Brooklyn boy, so you might not be safe in that outfit."

I didn't plan on walking far because I was carrying the bag containing my uniform. It was mid-March, and the weather was mild. As I started to walk away, I heard a voice beckoning to me.

"Hey, boy. I remembers you from Fort Laf'yet."

I turned around, and it was the Negro laborer who had been unloading the supply vessel at the fort a few weeks before and had cautioned the guard not to molest my trick-bag.

"Oh, I remember you."

"Let's us mosey over this-a-way. I needs to tell you something."

I was a bit leery of his intentions but decided to follow. Our refuge got us a bit away from the throngs of people moving to and fro.

"A few nights ago, I was caught something awful by a boo-hag. Couldn't breathe no how. Then I heard her whisper in my ear."

I began to understand what he was going to tell me.

"Do the name Vanita mean anything to you?" he asked.

"It might."

"Then you're Captain Jack?"

I was shocked to hear that name so far from home. I began to marvel at the range of Vanita's power.

"Yes, some call me that."

He let loose with a raucous laugh. "I seen some strange things when I was a slave, and I was teached to be afraid of hoodoo. Somes tried to tell me it was all just superstitions, but deep down, I knowed it was real. That's why I cautioned the guard about your bag. I see now I was wise to do it. Where is she?"

"Texas."

His eyes got wide, "She gots considerable powers."

"So what do you want?"

"I expecting maybe I should asks you what *you* want. She done told me to protect Captain Jack when he comes your way."

"Well, I will be leaving within two hours, so I don't reckon I have a need for much protecting. I was just set to explore a little before I board the ship."

"Ain't much to explore around here. Brooklyn and the rest of the boroughs are just New York. It's a mess of people and shops and factories all swirled together into a big pile. It ain't the healthiest place, but here a soul can pretty near disappear, though there are places a black man dare not go."

"You are a free man, right?"

"Well, escaped but free. But there's free and then there's *free*. Between the both of us, I'd say you're more likely the free man here, and you is still a prisoner."

At the time, I wasn't quite sure what he meant, but he put his hand on my shoulder and said, "Say, you must be hungry after that awful food in there."

"I could eat a horse."

"You got any money?"

"Just this ten-dollar gold piece the lieutenant gave me."

His eyes widened at the sight of it. "Put it away or somebody will steal it! I gots a little spending money. I 'spect your gold will do you more good down the road than it will here. I know a place nearby where we can get some bread and meat...enough for a quick meal." He stuck out his hand. "Name's Patrick. Used to be Silas, but I considered it my slave name. When I got north, I thought I needed a new name to go with my new life. Don't know why, just liked the name Patrick so I took it as my own. Maybe so people will cuss at me for being a Mick instead of my color."

"You can just call me Jack. 'Captain' doesn't set too well with the army."

"I don't imagine it do."

I followed Patrick through a maze of streets and shops until he found a small shop with what looked like meats and cheeses hanging in a window, and he thrust some coins in my hand, told me what to buy, and sent me in.

"They don't much like black folks shopping there, but the food is good. I gots a friend who usually goes in and gets me what I need."

I went in and procured the items he asked for. Once I had the food, we returned to the wharf near my ship, sat on some crates, and nibbled while he told me of his life.

"I grew up down in Virginny," he said. "The man who said he owned me wasn't so bad, I guess, and when I was a child, I didn't much know what was what. I first got an inkling of our situation was when one of my friends was suddenly just gone one day. My best friend Darius. Still don't know where he went. Sold, my mama told me. Then she cautioned me to not dwell on it 'cause it was the way of the world."

"I played with a lot of slave children down in Texas so I know what you are saying. At the time, I knew people called them slaves, but I didn't understand it all. Sometimes they just wouldn't be there anymore. Didn't know if they had died of the yellow fever or something else."

"Most probably sold," he said. "My mama raised me as a Christian, but I didn't see nothing Christian in the slavery. I mean, we had food and a roof but it…well, it just wasn't right, you know?"

"Yeah, it weighs on my mind sometimes."

"Another old slave who had run off a few times told me what to do. The last time he done run off, he had the back of his leg cut so he couldn't run no more. He could walk and he tended the massah's garden and grounds and such. This was long before this here war started. He showed me where the sun came up and told me it was east and if I faced the sun and turned this-a-way," he turned to his left, "then I was looking north. He told me *that* was the direction I needed to be headed."

"Easy enough," I said.

"Twarn't easy at all," he said. "When I kissed my mama bye and told her I was going to freedom, she cried and cried and begged me not to go. But I knowed it was what I needed to do. I left and never looked back. I was lucky in some respects since we lived not far from the skinniest bit of Maryland and there was just a spit of land before Pennsylvania and freedom. I expect slaves further down south have a much harder time. Still, I miss my mama, and every night, I say prayers to keep her safe. Didn't think about getting no hoodoo spell for protection, though. How'd that come about?"

"My mama died of a fever when I was twelve. My daddy, he always seemed to drink a lot of liquor, but after Mama died, he would just stay drunk and my life became unbearable. I left. I had to."

"Many a grief comes from the bottle."

"I know. That was living in Galveston."

Patrick raised his eyebrows. "I've heared of Galveston!"

"I managed to get as far as Houston. A widow woman there took pity on me and took me in, put me in charge of her slave, Old Moze."

Patrick instinctively leaned a little away from me at this statement. "You wuz a overseer?"

"Perhaps in principle, but I was thirteen, so it was mostly for appearances. Believe me, if anybody was in charge, it was Moze. He taught me how to ride, how to shoot, how to do most everything."

"How to shoot? Ain't never heard tell of any slave using a gun."

"Then a little over a year ago, Moze caught a chill and died. But before he died, he sent me off to find an old woman named Vanita."

"And she put the spell on you."

"I don't rightly understand it all, but it seems the truth of it. I'd met her before; I think she had some kind of hold on me even before that."

"Trick doctors got mysterious ways and powerful magic. Hah, but not powerful enough 'cause you gots captured."

"She warned me, at least I think she did. But, of course, I couldn't heed her warning because I was following orders."

"So's how did you end up in Laf'yet? Most Southerners they got in there seem to be blockade runners."

I shook my head. "I'm a soldier, a cavalryman. Moze knew of my intentions to sign up, and that's the real reason he sent for Vanita."

"So you fighting in this here war?" He seemed surprised.

"Not much fighting so far because there is so little war in Texas. I don't rightly know why I joined up. It seemed a proper thing to do. If Texas is in the war, I fight for Texas. From what I've seen, I have no fondness for slavery. Moze taught me that people are people. There are good ones and bad ones, whether they be white or black. But they are all people. There ain't anything I can do but remember what he taught me and live as best as I can. This little interlude has only shown me there ain't much to appreciate when being a prisoner, and I imagine being a prisoner ain't much different from being a slave."

"...'cepting maybe you going to be free soon of your own accord. Well, Jack, I don't much like the fact that you are fighting to keep my mama a slave, but I can surely respect a man who decides to stand up for his home. I see them recruiting Micks right off'n the boats, offering them cash money to put on the blue suit. They don't know what they's fighting for either. A meal, most likely."

"Vanita told me I was going to be fighting to free the slaves. She said she'd seen it because the South wasn't ever going to win this war, but it was necessary because slavery was never going to end without a fight."

"Ain't never heard it put like that."

We both looked up when a steamship whistle blew long and loud.

"It's your boat calling," he said. "You best be boarding now."

"Thanks for the food, Patrick. God bless you."

"You go on and lose the war for us," he said, chuckling as he ran down the street.

I shook his hand and headed down the dock to the waiting vessel, showed my release papers, and saluted the officer.

"Why, you're just a boy," he said. "Where did you serve and where and how were you captured?"

"Twenty-sixth Texas Cavalry, serving in Texas. Captured at Galveston on New Year's Day of this year," I said.

"How did you end up here?"

"I was caught between the lines in uniform, sir. I was trying to contact my father before the battle. He lived in Galveston." I added, "I had done it before, but this time I got captured by a patrol and was sent out to the blockading fleet before the battle had begun. Since then, no one has much known what to do with me, sir."

The officer laughed. "I can believe that. Do you have any other proof?"

I showed him my uniform in the bag and he nodded.

"I suggest you change back for your exchange. They're not too picky down there during exchanges, but they do respect a uniform."

"I understand."

I then boarded the vessel and joined with a few others bound for City Point in Virginia. I didn't mingle much during the passage. The weather was good and the seas were calm, and in twenty-four hours, I was standing on the dock at City Point in Virginia, signing my papers to allow for my reentry into the Confederate States. I wore my uniform with pride and informed the Confederate officers of my unit, rank, and my commander's name.

I was instructed to report to Richmond to get the necessary travel papers so I could return to Texas and the Twenty-Sixth Texas Cavalry.

Eighteen

Richmond was not quite as crowded as the city of New York, but being the center of the government for the Confederate States, it was quite impressive to a young soldier in uniform. It took me the better part of a day to find the office where I had been told to report. There was no shortage of bandaged men missing an arm or leg, sitting and begging for a means of getting something to eat. To a young soldier who had seen no combat, it was a sobering thing to behold. I was relieved when I found the place I was looking for.

"How did you come to be captured?" The question was directed at me by a stern major.

"General Magruder and Colonel DeBray had ordered me to perform some reconnaissance in Galveston prior to an attack. I lied to the Yankees and said I was trying to see my father. Well, it was not a total lie. I had already had some in contact with my father and hoped he might help provide me with information that would help us in our attack. I was picked up by a patrol before I could make contact with him."

"So you were acting as a spy," he said.

"I was in uniform, sir. General Magruder ordered it."

"What information do you have of New York?"

"I saw very little of it, sir. I was imprisoned in Fort Lafayette and then transported here when they released me. "

"Lafayette is used for political prisoners and privateers."

"Yes, sir. Since I was originally a prisoner of the blockading fleet, the Yankees never seemed to quite know what to do with me."

"And you want to get back to your unit, the Twenty-sixth Texas Cavalry?"

"Yes, sir."

"We need men here, you know, we could arrange for a transfer. We are going to whip the Yankees this coming year."

"Yes, sir, but I have trained with the Twenty-sixth. They are my comrades. Bring them here and we can all join the fight."

"You have a lot of spunk. I like that." He called out to an orderly, "Corporal, Private Benson here needs military travel documents and orders directing him to report back to the Twenty-sixth Texas Cavalry." Then he turned back and saluted me, "Private, good luck."

When I had the papers in hand, I had to make my own inquiries regarding transportation. In times of peace, I would imagine the trip would be better suited by ship, but I knew I could not depend upon the services of the blockading fleet for my return trip. I endeavored to find what land transportation I could. After many inquiries, I determined I might be able to take the railroad from Richmond south through North Carolina to Wilmington and by a circuitous route on through points west. I would have a hard time of it in Mississippi and beyond because it was said much of the area around the great river was under Union control. It seemed a daunting task to go so far, but I determined to try as best as I could.

I was never too proud to use my youth as an advantage, just as I did in my captivity. The railroads were in need of repair, which meant breakdowns and delays were common. I begged meals when we stopped, and I was always willing to do a variety of chores for temporary room and board. By the time I got to Montgomery, I was spent, both physically and financially. I found brief work in a livery stable, earning a little in the way of wages along with an allowance for food and a place to sleep.

Eventually, because of my experience with horses, I managed to sign on with a one-armed teamster named Fredericks who was carrying a load of supplies into Mississippi.

He slapped at the stub of his missing arm. "Lost it in Virginia in the first year of the war."

It was tough and slow work, and he cursed in ways I had hitherto never imagined. As it turned out, my experience with horses did not serve me well because mules are quite deserving of their stubborn reputation. This served as the chief inspiration for the colorful language Fredericks used in his own attempts to control them.

"I'm not a horseman, you see," he told me on the road, "I'm a mule-skinner. These beasts are stout and strong, but they take the singular skills of a mule-skinner to coax them on their way."

I did not particularly like the work and, in truth, he didn't really need me, but I think he craved some human company on the road. Working with him served my purposes and kept my belly full. I soon learned enough to prove my worth.

I never knew his first name; he and everyone we met only called him Fredericks. He was a stout man about my height with a massive bushy beard, and his one muscled forearm was twice normal size. He was as boisterous in his communications with travelers as he was with his mules. I learned later that mule-skinners relished their reputation for colorful language.

Military activity along the roads of Mississippi was quite evident, and there was much local concern with the Yankee actions against a place called Vicksburg. Although I had not mentioned any of my particulars to him, Fredericks seemed to understand my predicament and advised me to take leave of his team in mid-Mississippi. He was headed to Jackson, but from what he had heard, if I veered toward Natchez, I might manage to stay out of trouble if I wore civilian clothes and travelled carefully on foot.

"You'll have to have a heap of luck to find passage across the river," he said, adding, "and watch out for them Yankee gunboats."

After I told him good-bye, he lamented losing me. "You learned to handle the team with some skill." Then he added, "But you'll never be considered much of a mule-skinner because you haven't the vocabulary for it."

Fredericks paid me in gold coin because, he said, he liked me and wanted to see me get on home. I swear, this gruff old man had a tear in his eye as I told him goodbye.

"You didn't have to help me," I told him as I started to walk to the west, "but I appreciate everything you've done for me."

"Aye, but I *did* have to help you. Godspeed, Captain Jack," he said.

I turned around to ask him what he meant, but he had already lurched away, snapping his whip and cursing at his mules in ways that would make the coarsest seaman blush.

I walked to the west on foot. Meals were not hard to come by because I could always manage to earn some food by chopping wood at farmhouses. This was because most of the menfolk were either off fighting the war or they were already infirm or dead from it. This was the place where I saw for myself the privations this war was putting on the people. It was in stark contrast to the land of plenty I had witnessed up north.

The army seemed splendid and all when we were parading and I had been mightily impressed by the hustle and bustle of Richmond. I knew now those activities were only shadows in the background of the war. Here on the backroads of Mississippi there was another story being written and it was one of hardship. I wondered if any of these poor people would ever recover anything akin to a normal state of existence, no matter who won the war. After what I had seen, the sacrifices did not seem worth the effort.

I managed to put away a sack of extra food as I got closer to the river. I was somewhat south of Natchez when I managed to stumble up one of the levees in the light of a full moon and beheld the massive river that gave the state its name. The size of it was intimidating. I hid my trick bag in a tree and dozed nearby under the stars, and as I slept, I was occasionally awakened by the sounds of steam engines heavily straining against the current. I knew I was hearing the sound of Union boats running up the river.

As I dozed, I dreamed of a hand on my shoulder.

"Boss," was the whispered word I heard in my dreams.

"Boss."

This time I woke up, and I lifted my head to see a blurred face framed by the full moon it was blocking.

"Is you Captain Jack?"

That snapped me wide-awake like a slap in the face.

"Who are you?"

"Name's Johnny. Some kinda magic made me come and find you. Hag-ridden, I 'spect. I couldn't catch my breath until I heard the words in mah mind, and I knew I had ta come finds you."

"And do what, turn me over to the Yankees?"

"No, suh. I gots me a canoe hereabouts. I thinks I supposed to paddle you across this river with it, if'n you can help me haul it a ways back up the river on ta otha side."

"I can do that. Where'd you get a canoe?"

"Suh, we call this here the river of plenty. If'n you prowl around the riverbanks, theyz no telling watchu gonna find. It were a might ragged when I grabbed it, but I patched it up. Gets me some good catfish with it, too, from time to time."

I quickly gathered my belongings, including my trick-bag, and followed as Johnny led me about a mile up river and then showed me where he had secreted his canoe. It indeed looked a little worse for the wear, but he showed me that it held out the water and was a sturdy little craft. I knew nothing about canoes, but Johnny proved to be an expert. He gave me a brief instruction in the use of his crude oars.

"Ah fashioned dese here oars mahsef," he said proudly. "You hold it like this," he showed me how he grabbed his, one hand high, one hand low, "and then you push down from the side I ain't paddling."

We shoved off from the riverbank and he paddled hard against the current, trying to lose as little ground as he could. The river was clear of gunboats at present.

"Don't usually see none o' those big boats this time o' the morning" he said. "One or two makes a run 'bout midnight, then it's calm until daybreak."

We probably lost a mile or two to the current, but in a short time, we made it across. On the other shore, I helped Johnny pull the boat up the levee.

"I figure I done this here about a hunnert times."

Together, we hoisted the canoe over our heads and walked up the levee about two miles where we put it back down.

We rested a minute together before Johnny began his return trip.

"Captain Jack, can I asks you a question?"

"Of course."

"Who IS you? And why is some witch woman haunting me to help you?"

"It's a tough question to answer. Basically, I'm just a Southern soldier. An old friend of mine, Moze, asked her to look after me to help protect me."

"She's got the hoodoo, ain't she?" he asked.

"That's what they say."

"Will she leave me alone now?"

"I suppose. Had she ever bothered you before?"

"No, suh! Dis chere the first time."

"Maybe she'll throw you some good luck for helping me," I said. "But I don't rightly know."

"Well, suh, tell her I helped you go and she can leave me alone from now on. Now you best git before them bluecoats sees you," he said, shaking my hand.

My last sight of Johnny after I pushed him into the big river was him paddling against the current as he made his way to the other side.

~ * ~

I knew there were probably Yankee patrols closer to Vicksburg, but Fredericks said he had heard they were not as strong this far south. I knew I needed to head directly west as quickly as possible. I had perhaps another hour of darkness, so I pushed on, assuming even a few miles would take me closer to my goal.

As the first rays of the sun were just beginning the stretch across the sky, I decided I had better find some refuge. If the Yankees were patrolling around here, I knew I had better lay low during the day and travel at night until I knew I was in lands free from their intrusions.

"Suh!" came a whisper from the shadows.

"Who's there?"

It was a black woman, perhaps forty and plump, with her hair tied with a rag.

"Is you Captain Jack?"

"Yes." I knew Vanita was still following me.

"Come to me in a nightmare... couldn't breathe... after that I knew had to come helps you."

"Hag-rider?"

"I reckon so. Okay, Captain Jack, so just who is you?"

"I am trying to get back to Texas but need to hide from the Yankees."

"I gots a place you can sleep. Old cabin in the woods not too far from here. Follow me."

I followed the woman through the woods about another mile and saw the shack. It wasn't much but it was hidden. Inside, there was an old moth-eaten straw mattress.

"You got food?"

"I have some. I appreciate the help."

"I suggests you go up yonder," she said, pointing to a loft. "Dem bluecoats is a nosy lot. Dey might come looking in here. Out of sight, out of mind, my mama always said."

I tested the crude ladder, and it seemed sturdy so I climbed. There was a pile of hay up there as well.

"Me and Maurice sometimes comes here for a little private time," she said with a laugh, "so, come dark, you better skedaddle."

"I will."

"I'll try to bring you some vittles to take wit' you. Just don't wants no mo' witchwomans whispering in my ear."

I stretched out on the hay and was soon sound asleep.

Come nightfall, she returned as promised with a bag of hoe cakes and a gourd of water.

"Best as ah kin do."

"It is fine," I said.

She took me outside and instructed me where to go next. I had to trust in any fear Vanita might have instilled in the woman. I thanked her profusely for her help and got on my way. The rising moon behind me told me she had correctly directed me west, and I knew I would soon be out of the Yankee-controlled territory.

Although I still had a considerable distance to cross, I knew I was on my way home.

Nineteen

I encountered a wagon driven by a young boy not long before dawn.

"Can you tell me something?"

"Depends on what it is."

"Are there any Yankee troops around here?"

"Yankees?"

"Yes," I said.

"No Yankees here," he said, "they are all to the east. Oh, there might be a patrol or two, but our boys usually chase them off."

"Thank you."

"You a Yankee?"

"No, not at all, but I'm a long way from home. I was a Yankee prisoner for a while, and I'm trying to get back to Texas."

"There's a group of soldiers about five miles from here. Head up to the crossroads and go to the west," he said.

I was quite pleased to receive this information. I changed back into my uniform and marched forward to try to find the soldiers in the hope I could hasten my pace back to Texas.

I followed the boy's directions, continuing to walk through the morning even though I was tired from my long journey the night before. I had been in the habit of sleeping during the day, which meant it was getting nigh on to my bedtime, but I found I had a renewed vigor as I approached what I hoped was a Confederate camp.

Finally, I spied a gray-clad picket a little ways off, and a sweeter sight I had not beheld in a long time. I approached with my hands up and called out.

"Halloo!"

"Who goes there!"

"Private Benson with the Twenty-sixth Texas Cavalry," I said.

"Texas? This here's Louisiana."

"I know that. I was captured and exchanged and am trying to get back to my company."

"You got any papers?"

"Yes," I said and I approached the sentry and handed him my papers. He gave them only a cursory glance.

"Don't do me much good since I cain't read nohow," he said. "My relief is due here soon, and I'll take you to the sergeant."

"I'm much obliged," I said. "I've been traveling all night to hide from Yankee patrols. You mind if I just rest while we wait?"

"Help yourself," he said.

I sat with my back against a nearby tree and promptly fell asleep. I don't know how long I was out, but I was soon awakened by a shake.

"Let's go, my relief is here." It was the original sentry, joined by another.

I rousted myself and followed the soldier up the road where a ragged squad-sized group was camped. We approached a tent where a sergeant was in the process of shaving.

"Sergeant, this man says he is a soldier. He approached my picket post. Says he is on his way back to his unit in Texas."

"Texas? What unit?"

I spoke up. "Twenty-sixth Texas Cavalry."

"Where's your horse, cavalryman?" he laughed.

"I hope he's still with my unit," I said. "I was captured at Galveston when Magruder recaptured the city. I was dismounted at the time."

"I see. And do you have any orders?"

"Yes," I said, handing the sergeant my paper. "I showed it to the sentry."

"Unfortunately, Private Champaign can't read a word."

He put the razor down and read my papers carefully.

"All the way from Virginia?" He looked at me, astonished. "How in heaven's name did you cross the river?"

"A kindly Negro had a canoe he had salvaged and he took me across," I said. "We managed to get across without encountering any Union gunboats," I added.

"Amazing," he said. "What's in the bag?"

"Civilian clothes. A gift from the wife and daughter of one of my jailors."

"Where were you held?"

"New York City," I said, "at Fort Lafayette."

"New York?"

"Yes. I was captured as I was scouting the city, and they sent me out to the blockade fleet just as the battle was beginning. They really didn't quite know what to do with me."

He looked at me closely by the light of his lantern. "You're just a boy."

"Been a soldier more than a year. My youth worked in my favor," I said. "Like these clothes, I think they were using them, trying to lure me away from the army."

"Then they would just conscript you at a later date."

"So I assumed," I said. "They also offered to let me enlist, but I declined."

"You eaten?"

"Not since yesterday," I said. "Some slave woman bequeathed me a gift of hoe cakes."

"Salt beef and dried corn is all we have. It is the life blood of this army."

"It sounds like home," I said.

The sergeant finished his shave and pulled on his shirt and uniform coat. "Let's get you some vittles," he said, "and I might just have a surprise for you."

As we approached a small group of soldiers, I could smell smoke and the aroma of burned fat. A private was frying up a quantity of salt beef, and when it was sufficiently fried, he removed it and toasted the parched corn in the salty grease and added a quantity of water to make some mush. It was similar to rations I had eaten in my own camp and on my long journey as well. As we ate, I explained a bit more of my own service in the cavalry. They were much impressed by the story of my encounter with shore-bound blockaders and even more amazed at the tale of my two incursions into the environs of Yankee-held Galveston.

"Of course, we have had some minor contacts with the Yankees, being as they are so close," said the sergeant, who told me his name was Gindrat, pronounced gin-DRAH in the French fashion. "A few days ago, a scouting party of Yankee cavalry came close by, and Private Bouchart over there took a potshot at them. Wounded one of them and he fell off his horse. He was picked up by someone in his unit, but his danged horse ran off. We've heard it not far away, but every time any of us have tried to approach, it's run off."

As if by providence, I heard a horse cry out.

"See? There he is."

"Give me some rope and a few handfuls of dried corn," I said. "Maybe I can get him for you. He sounds hungry to me. I imagine those Yankee horses are used to being fed regularly."

The sergeant complied, and we quietly moved off in the direction of the sound. He was not far off, obviously stalking the camp in hopes of a handout, or so I thought. I walked within fifty feet of the animal.

"He's a nice piece of horse flesh," the sergeant said.

I talked gentle soothing horse talk to him, coaxing him and gently assuring him I meant no harm. I say him, but when I was close enough, I perceived it was a filly.

"Come on, girl, I won't hurt you, look what I have for you."

I showed the horse the grain and got her attention. I had looped one end of the rope before approaching. I knew this was a broken riding horse, not a wild horse, so I assumed the sight of a rope or a man would not spook her.

Still, she was wary of strangers and seemed nervous as I slowly walked up. She listened to the soothing sound of my voice and eyed those precious grains of corn. She likely needed water as well, and I wished I had carried a bucket with me. I had what I had and it would have to do. I finally got close enough and reached out my hand, and her lips stretched out ever so cautiously to pull at the grains of corn in my outstretched hand. After the first few grains, she greedily ate the rest. I had filled my pockets at the camp, so I slowly got another handful and she did not hesitate at all to devour another helping. On the third handful, I slowly lowered the loop of rope around her neck, then gave her another handful. I was almost out of corn, but I had the rope firmly in hand. If she chose to walk with us to get more corn, we had her. Of course, she could just bolt, and there was no way I could hold her if she did that.

To my great relief, she walked with me until I managed to secure her to a tree, where I let her drink her fill from a bucket and eat a little more corn. The squad did not have much to spare, but they were happy to donate some of their supply to the cause.

Sergeant Gindrat said, "If I wasn't completely sure I believed your story before, I believe you now. You definitely know your way around horses."

"She's nice, just lonely. A horse trained to work for humans really craves the friendship and companionship, even if they might be a little afraid of strangers. You just have to show them you mean no harm."

"We're going to be relieved at this outpost later today and go back to our main camp," he said. "I'm going to recommend to the captain that we give this horse to you. Hell, they'll probably just want to eat her. We are meat starved."

"Eat her?" I was alarmed. "She's a great horse."

"We're infantry, and a horse is just another mouth to feed. I'm going to show him your papers and say she belongs to you fair and square. Besides, a cavalryman needs a horse. She looks healthy. She'll help get you back to where you need to go."

I doubted whether the captain would give her to me, but while I removed her saddle and rubbed the rough areas where the leather had been cinched tight, I enjoyed a few fantasy visions of me riding back to Company K on a splendid Yankee mount. I could tell she was happy to be relieved of her burden and seemed to relish the attention I was giving to her.

I dozed around their camp until the noon hour when the sound of some footfalls announced the approach of this squad's relief. The other sergeant spied the Yankee horse and asked, "How'd you get the horse?"

Sergeant Gindrat answered, "Yankee patrol dropped it."

"The captain will be impressed."

"We couldn't get near her, but this private, a lost cavalryman on his way back to his unit in Texas, coaxed her to join us."

"Texas! Good job, Texas!"

"Thank you."

As the squad's pickets came in and we prepared to march back to their main camp, Sergeant Gindrat said to me, "It would be a shame to walk this fine horse back to our camp, why don't you ride her, Jack?"

"You mean it?"

"Yes."

"Is it far?" I asked the sergeant.

"Not too far. Several miles," he said.

"I'm not sure if it is a good idea. She'd been wearing her saddle for days and she might not take to it yet. A horse can't be wearing them for days and days…it's much the same as us needing to take our shoes off."

"It would be easier to control her."

"Perhaps," I said, and I retrieved the blanket and tack. I checked the fittings, set the bridle, then replaced and cinched the saddle. She showed no sign of countering my actions. I mounted her and rode her down the road and back. I could tell the poor horse was a might worrisome at carrying an unfamiliar rider.

"I'll ride her a ways but might walk her part of the way. She likely still has some tender spots from wearing the saddle so long."

We proceeded down the road. She was a good horse, and as she got used to my touch, she became quite responsive to my use of the bridle. The lack of spurs was not an issue in her handling. I entertained a measure of respect for the Yankees; I could tell she had been well-trained and her trooper had taken good care of her. I liked riding her, but I could tell she wanted to be relieved of her saddle and bridle for a while.

I dismounted when we approached the larger camp. It was a unit not much different from Company K, except that it was infantry, not cavalry. After I had secured the animal and relieved her of her burdens, the sergeant and I went off to meet the captain.

Captain Beauchamp was a tall, imposing figure. He read my orders and welcomed me graciously to his camp. "I have a very high regard for General Magruder," he said, "and was much impressed with his actions in pushing those damned Yankees off our precious Galveston. With those interlopers in possession of portions of our fair state, it was indeed good to hear he had saved Texas from the same fate."

"We were all anxious to reclaim it," I said and proceeded to explain a bit of my own part prior to the battle of Galveston. I then told him the story of my imprisonment and trip to New York, then my return as an exchanged prisoner. At this point, the sergeant recounted how I aided them in capturing their squad's war prize. The captain stood and accompanied us to examine the horse up close.

"An excellent animal," he said.

Sergeant Gindrat addressed the officer, "Sir, the boys and me think we should give the horse to young Private Benson here. He is a cavalryman, sir, and this horse will greatly enhance his travels back to his unit in Texas."

"That's a fine idea, Sergeant. We really have no fodder for another horse besides mine. In truth, from what you both told me, he rightly captured the prize."

Then he looked at me and continued. "But I very much like this Yankee saddle. Mine is a bit worn. I wonder if you might be willing to trade saddles with me."

I responded, "How can I refuse?" and accepted the other saddle sight unseen.

After a day's rest in their camp for both me and the horse, who I had started calling Prize, I assembled a few supplies granted to me by the captain. Prize didn't have any serious defects and had suffered no bad sores as a result of her long confinement in saddle and bridle. I knew it would take her a little time to get used to a new saddle—it always does, a bit like a man breaking in a new pair of shoes—but the used saddle would likely be a quick transition for her. The horse was branded with marks that identified her as Union property, so the captain drafted papers detailing her capture as a war prize and at what point and by what circumstances she had come into my possession.

"Of course, I doubt the Yankees will accept this as ownership, but it might preclude them from executing you as a horse thief if you are captured."

After handshakes all around, I bid my new friends adieu and, with my growing stock of papers in my bag, I rode off toward Texas. Prize was a good horse, and she carried me the entire way with no problem. The captain had given me a small stipend, and by a combination of this money, along with a few chores, the good graces of the fine citizens of Louisiana and East Texas, and luck, I got myself back to Houston, where I entered the headquarters of the Houston District of the Department of the Trans-Mississippi. I soon found myself in an office, facing Colonel DeBray himself.

Twenty

Colonel DeBray examined my papers with great interest; he did not recognize me at first. I knew he was a busy man, but the strain of his war duties was evident in his demeanor. Then he seemed to hesitate in reading the papers, and he looked up with a start as it suddenly dawned on him who I was.

"Private Benson?"

"Yes, sir!"

Then he made some exclamation in French I did not understand and broke his usual stern military protocol. Standing up and grasping me on both shoulders, he pulled me to him and kissed me on both cheeks.

"We thought you were gone forever," he said. "We knew you had been captured because your father reported that fact to us but... well..."

He invited me to sit, and I related the story of my adventure. He listened as I told him about my capture, the long voyage to New York, my incarceration, the exchange at City Point, my time in Richmond, and my long journey to the west.

"How did Richmond seem?"

"It is a center of activity. Not nearly as bustling as New York, but surely they are busy with the war."

"I can't understand why every request I've made to be transferred east has been denied. It is as if some unseen force is intent on keeping us here."

As it was getting onto noon, he insisted I take lunch with him and asked me what seemed like a hundred questions about my experiences. He expressed the most interest in how I managed to traverse the big river, and when we finished dining, he came down and inspected Prize.

"The Yankees are certainly not lacking in quality horses. She is indeed a fine cavalry horse."

After he spoke with his aide, he informed me of the location of the Twenty-sixth and provided me with new orders, which were dated for the next day.

He gave me some money. "I insist you stay at the Fannin Hotel in town tonight as my guest. Mention my name, and they will make sure you have a room. Texas owes you much for your service, but unfortunately, this is the best I can do, and this is out of my own pocket. Sleep in a bed tonight, have a good meal, and let your new horse have her fill of hay at the livery."

I bade the colonel farewell and proceeded to find myself a room for the night. Prize was boarded in luxury and soon I was, too. The hotel's dining fare was limited, but the taste of some good Texas beef did much to cure me of the ills of my long privations. I took a slow walk after dinner and enjoyed watching all of the activity of the Houston streets. I remembered the crowds and bustle of New York and Richmond and contrasted those places with Houston but there was no comparison.

I was jostled out of these daydreams by the sudden appearance of a firm hand upon my shoulder. I turned around and was immediately taken aback. Vanita stood there, staring through me with her cloudy eye. She was in the company of a young slave boy.

"Captain Jack," she whispered. "I'se been expecting you. Glad to see you've come home from your long journey."

I was still fearful of her, though in this instant I was more startled by her unexpected appearance.

"Let me see your trick bundle," she said. "I knows you still gots it. Let me see it!"

I pulled the red flannel bag out of my trouser pocket and handed it to her. She held it in both palms and put it to her face as if to sniff it. Then she put it to her breast and lowered her head and mumbled a few words I could not understand.

"You'ze done as I asked, kept it all ready. Its power is still full, even more powerful." She put it back in my hands.

"Do I ever need to use anything out of it?"

"No. It is just mostly to keep you safe by you knowing it's there. I'll let you know if'n I needs it to do anything else. Tuck it back away, quick."

I complied, stuffing it into my pocket.

"My messengers have all done their work, so you are still safe and sound."

"Yes."

"Good. I see more struggles and danger for you, boy, but you are strong. The spirit of Moze done serves you as much as the powers of the bag. I've given you more help than you can even know." She patted me haphazardly on the shoulder that bore her mark. "Now I best be on my way. Godspeed, Captain Jack."

She pulled at her young charge and headed away from me, moving forward in stops and starts down the muddy street. I blinked away a tear and remembered the cursing, one-armed muleskinner Fredericks's identical parting words.

Encounters with Vanita, both real and imagined, always unnerved me, and it took me a few minutes to refresh my thoughts. I made my way to my hotel where I slept soundly from the early evening to the next morning in the luxuriating comfort of a real bed.

I was awakened by a knocking at my door. I cautiously opened it, expecting the proprietor or perhaps someone seeking me out to prematurely prod me back to my army service but was quite surprised to see my father standing there.

"Jack!"

"Pa!"

"Colonel DeBray telegraphed me in Galveston, informing me of your safe return. I made an early trip up by steamer this morning."

I quickly dressed and we were soon downstairs, feasting on eggs and some gamey bacon I assumed was made from wild hog. I again related the experiences of my captivity and liberation and of my long journey.

"It is a miracle you have survived this. I thank the Lord that you are returned."

As he said this, a vision of Vanita appeared in my head, and I wondered if the Lord had as much to do with my salvation as the old trick-doctor.

I grabbed my few belongings and left the hotel with my father before we went to pick up Prize from the stable. Pa marveled at the sight of her.

"What a fine steed. The luck was certainly with you."

I knew luck had little to do with it. It was Moze's training that had helped rescue the poor horse from its predicament, but it was always a hard thing to explain.

He helped me prepare Prize for the trip and, all too soon, I was ready to go rejoin Company K and the rest of the Twenty-sixth.

"Stay safe, Jack. Don't ever take such a risk again."

"Pa, I'm in the cavalry, I have to follow my orders."

He looked down. "I know, son, I know."

I mounted Prize and made my way down the muddy streets of rain-soaked Houston, looking back and waving at Pa as he stood alone, watching me go.

As I reached the outskirts of town, the clouds broke and the sun came out to warm me on the rest of my journey. I could smell the smoke from the many fires at the encampment before I saw it. Sentries stopped me on the road and examined my papers, saw they had been signed by Colonel DeBray, and motioned me on my way, directing me to the camp of Company K. I saw Captain Hare's tent and a few familiar faces, most of whom stopped and stared as if they were seeing a returned spirit. The captain emerged from his tent just as I approached and seemed to suffer the same fate as the others, standing for a moment with his mouth open. The spell was broken when I dismounted and saluted him.

"Private Benson reporting for duty, sir."

He recovered sufficiently to return the salute and then said, "Jack! I just don't know what to say. It is a miracle to see you again. We thought you were lost to the war, or worse."

One of the lieutenants procured extra chairs, and I again related the details of my journey, answering questions along the way. They were both quite in awe of my experiences.

I was directed to my squad, and I steeled myself for yet another rendition of my experiences. I sometimes wished I could print up an itinerary of my travels so I could be relieved of this tedious recitation.

"Private Benson," came a sound off to my right. I turned and saw the visage of Sergeant Murphy. "It is so nice of you to rejoin us. Did you have a nice furlough?"

"Sergeant! I can assure you I've been on no furlough!"

He slapped me on the back, marveled at the fine lines of Prize, and led me over to where the horses were quartered. I procured her some fodder, and she introduced herself to the other mounts. I scanned the enclosure but did not see Elvira.

"Where's Elvira?"

Sergeant Murphy, usually poker-faced and sullen, let his features grow soft and he toed the ground with his boot. "She fell ill shortly after you disappeared. I don't know if a horse can die from a broken heart, but it's the only explanation I can offer. We had a long spate of bad weather, and she caught a chill she could not shake off. The boys all took turns taking care of her. They tried their best."

This saddened me to no end, but as I looked over to Prize, I knew Elvira's replacement would serve me just as well. She had gotten used to me on the last leg of our journey, and we were quite bonded as a pair. I began brushing the road dust off her coat, and she nuzzled me, as if she felt the pain of my sense of loss. She snorted at the other horses for their condolences and they all snorted back.

"Seems to me as if that Yankee filly is fitting right in with our good Southern stock," the sergeant said.

With Prize taken care of, he took me over to the squad where I first encountered Rufus and Robert White. They both initially pretended to pay me no notice. Then they broke from their joke, laughing heartily.

"We'd already heard the news, old man. Welcome home," Robert said.

We all shook hands, patted each other on the back, and hooted and hollered to no end. It was time for noon mess, and as I reunited with all the old crew, they sat me down and I regaled them all with the tale of my capture and long journey, totally prepared for a new onslaught of questions.

I felt slightly out of place, having been gone for five months, but so much had changed. I was still in my dirty old greys, and they were resplendent in red flannel shirts and new trousers. They looked quite different, even older and more wizened, but I knew they were still the same old boys I had known since our service first started.

Everyone wanted to see Prize, and I was quite proud to show her off. They had preserved my old saddle, and I bequeathed my current saddle to a fellow in another squad, who Rufus said he knew was struggling with a horribly cracked and worn saddle. He offered me a few dollars he had been saving to get himself a new one, but since the saddle had cost me nothing, I just let him have it.

I was soon marched off to the quartermaster to see if I could be decked out like the rest of the company. Lieutenant Mason was now serving as the quartermaster, and he looked me up and down. "Private Benson, returned from the dead," he said and followed with, "tsk, tsk, tsk."

Then from some hidden spot among his supplies, he pulled out garments in the same style. "I don't know, Private, I had just an inkling you would be returning to us, so I put these aside for that eventuality."

I smiled from ear to ear.

Then he pulled out a Halls carbine...MY halls, and then the Enfield. "These were turned in to me after you disappeared. Again,

I just had a feeling. Seemed a shame to waste them on someone else. You are the best shot in the regiment."

He also produced a Colt Navy revolver. "Come to think of it, perhaps you can find a good home for this, captured at Galveston. I think you've earned this bit of war prize."

I was elated as I left his tent with my new outfit and armed to the teeth. I was soon attired just like my comrades, and just as soon, the sergeant approached me and announced it was high time I got back into the routine of regular army life. I was ordered to dig a new latrine trench and fill in the old one. Rufus was pronounced my partner in crime, and we got right to work. It was a little strange being back, but in no time at all, the routines became second nature. In the outside world, this was an unimaginable existence, but when a soldier is among his comrades once again, anything seems possible.

Twenty-one

I had been absent from Company K for only a little more than five months, but it had seemed like a lifetime. As the days ran into weeks and then became additional months, the monotony of army life began to seem like yet another lifetime. We were kept busy by continuing to drill, keeping up with the duties of camp life, and of course there were regular patrols. The blockaders were more brazen every month, always seeking fresh meat and water.

After seeing a bit of the rest of the Confederacy during my travels, I knew how good we had it in Texas. We had plenty of meat and there was food, but stockpiles of other items were low. I had actually begun to enjoy my daily ration of coffee in captivity. Now it was a rare item indeed. What little we received through Mexico was expensive, and it was worth far more in Virginia than it was in Texas. In fact, this was a problem with almost everything. Speculators and smugglers knew if they could get things across the Mississippi, they could almost name their own price. This speculation began to deprive us of even the minor luxuries we had known so well.

Many in the Twenty-sixth complained because we were out of the action, but in Richmond, I had seen the aftermath of war. The wounded veterans of many of our campaigns were convalescing almost everywhere I looked, and I wondered if the South would be able to supply the country's demand for crutches and bandages. The suffering I had witnessed was immense, for the cruelties of war are many. I secretly wondered if Vanita's statement, that she had given me more help than I could know, meant she had some hand in our continued assignment to the Texas coast.

On sentry duty one long night, Rufus asked me about New York City.

"Is it as big and crowded as they say?"

"Well," I said, "I must admit, I saw only a small portion of it, but that portion was more crowded and busier than anyplace I've ever seen in my life."

Rufus seemed suitably impressed.

"And I'll tell you the thing I found most amazing," I said. "Although I was imprisoned by the army in an old fort, from what I saw, the city seems untouched by the war."

"How is that?"

"I mean, although there are naval ships in the harbor and more than a few uniforms on the street, the general feeling of the city was... *normal.* The conversations and the daily comings and goings seemed like it was the same as it had likely always been. Most of the talk I heard was talk about business and talk about life. The newspapers I managed to read spoke of the war but, well...the war seemed very far away."

"Far away? They don't care about this war?"

"As near as I could tell, they only care about the parts that line their pockets with federal greenbacks."

"We should build an ironclad and go in and shell the city," Rufus said.

"I think it would make nary an impact on the throngs of busy souls I saw there. It would be swallowed up whole."

"What are you saying, Jack?"

"I don't know, Rufus. I don't think we can ever hope to win this here war."

"Don't say such a thing!"

"I saw Richmond as well, don't forget. Now there, everything was all about the war, but New York was nonchalant about the whole thing. Attitudes are different. When you think about the battles in Virginia, those folks in New York are far closer to the action than we are, but they are almost completely removed from the whole thing. The numbers of people, the factories, the supplies, and the ships coming in with even more goods. How can we ever hope to fight against all of that?"

Rufus looked down, lost in thought. "I never thought about it."

"Best we can do, I suppose, is to just keep training and hope we can keep up the good fight. The Yankees I saw, the army I mean, seem more concerned about comfort than deprivation. If General Lee can give them a good fight in the East and if Pemberton can continue to hold Vicksburg, maybe they'll lose their taste for this war. It's our only chance. Some I talked to sounded tired of the war, I know that."

"I hear rumors General Lee is set to whup the Yankees for good this spring."

"From what I saw, Richmond was a mountain of activity. But I also saw many wounded men. Let me tell you, there were a lot of them in Richmond, many missing arms or legs."

Conversations seemed to go like this every night and at every mess because boredom was a soldier's constant companion. The monotony of camp life began to wear heavily on the troops. The officers drilled us even harder to try to relieve it.

Ball games filled in some of our time. It was easy to play in the small places allotted to us, and it was great fun swatting at what balls we could make out of cowhide. Some preferred card games, especially at night. Music was a source of joy for many, and most nights, one could hear a strumming banjo and singing.

There may be glory in battle, but there is no glory in trying to live out one's life in a soldier's role. We cherished every opportunity we were given to mount up and go on patrols, perform dispatch duty, or to carry supplies. Even latrine duty, as disgusting as it was, gave a chance to do something to relieve the overbearing drudgery of the camp.

Good news came not long after my discussion with Rufus. This was not a rumor, this was real news...a huge battle with the Yankees had been won.

Robert told me with a whoop, "Chancellorsville! We whipped them Yankees! Fighting Joe Hooker was soundly defeated!"

There was much rejoicing in camp to hear this. We hoped perhaps the war was on a downward slope. This meant two resounding victories in a row, and Vicksburg still stood firm against the Federal siege. I had, of course, seen and heard the many gunboats on the Mississippi, but they could only go so far, it was said, because the Confederate guns at Vicksburg would turn them back. These constant rumors made emotions run high in camp.

Then came devastating news.

The sergeant shared it with us at roll call. "Stonewall Jackson has been martyred to the cause," he said.

He had been cut down in the heat of the battle at Chancellorsville. The high feelings of the past days were snuffed like one would smother a candle. Still, our officers and sergeants would tell us, General Lee was still there, and Longstreet and Jeb Stuart, but the legendary exploits of General Jackson inspired us all. It was a hard loss to accept.

In the following weeks, more rumors flowed. That is an interesting thing about army life. Rumors come from every direction and sometimes they are just silly.

"I heard the Yankees are planning an invasion at Indianola..."

"General Grant was found face down in the Mississippi..."

And then there would be yet another rumor to refute the one before. But one rumor did prove true: the one about General Lee moving north to take the war to the Yankees.

The bad thing about Texas is that with Louisiana basically split by the Yankees, true news was especially slow to reach us. As the drenching rains of the late spring moved into the blistering heat of the high summer, we heard rumors of Lee taking Philadelphia or Washington. I could not imagine these cities being "taken" if they were any bit as immense and unconcerned with the war as New York had been.

Then came the devastating news to add to the oppressive heat of the summer. I had just returned from a patrol to the coast. The constant winds blowing off the Gulf of Mexico had served as a refreshing respite from the blistering heat inland.

Rufus held his head down as he said, "Pemberton has surrendered to Grant at Vicksburg."

This did not seem possible, but Grant's siege had starved the city into submission. The great river was now a Yankee highway cutting right through the heart of our country. I had seen the gunboats sailing the river with my own eyes, so I knew how imposing they were.

Then from the east came news of a great battle at a little crossroads in Pennsylvania named Gettysburg.

The entire company was called to parade and Captain Hare told us about it.

"We have reports about three days of horrific battle with many casualties. General Lee's army is intact but weakened, and he has returned to Virginia."

News was scarce, but our overall feeling was that, without Stonewall Jackson, Lee's planned invasion of the North was simply not possible. For once, I wished a rumor had not been true.

When I heard this, I knew the cause was lost. It was no matter, though. I had signed up fair and square, and I was resolute in my conviction to stay in this army until the end. I was resolved not to let my comrades down. I had not suffered the privations of capture and incarceration, not to mention the hardships of returning from New York all the way to Texas, to become a deserter.

Secession? I never fully understood it, and the more I knew of slavery, the less I liked it. So in my heart, I didn't have much of a reason to stick around, but I was in the army and I knew it was my sworn duty to uphold my word. I was a bit shy of seventeen, but I knew I was as much a man as anyone.

In solitary moments, I would conjure up images of sweet Pearl and fondly remember our conversations. I sighed as I touched the part of my cheek she had kissed. Sometimes I would unfold the handkerchief and outline the dainty P embroidered in the corner. These moments weakened my resolution, but I would not give in.

Life in our army continued along these lines as word reached us of new battles at places like Lookout Mountain and Chickamauga. Rumors of Southern victories were quickly tainted by the revised news of huge losses. I had seen portions of both the north and the south with my own eyes. When we lost men, they were lost for good, but when the Yankees lost men, there was a seemingly endless supply of new bodies to replace them. I remembered Patrick telling me of immigrants signing up to fight right as they came off the boats in New York harbor.

Patrols were our only relief from the drudgery of camp life and the bleak news from the real war. I had another brief hint of war on one of those patrols along the coast. It was very similar to the earlier patrol. Our path was now familiar; we knew the stops and we knew the lay of the land. In the still of the night, I was on picket duty and could hear the rhythmic splashes of oars slapping at the water. We had seen the lights of a steamer offshore and had suspected it was a brazen blockader coming in close for a look. In Virginia, North Carolina, or South Carolina, there might be artillery available to scare off such an interloper, but on the long and desolate Texas coastline, cannons were in short supply. I kept watch while Robert White went to wake the corporal. It was a shore party sure enough, probably in search of beef to plunder for their mess. It seemed they would never learn. I had my Enfield with me. It took a bit longer to load than the Halls, but it was much more accurate at a longer distance. I had only a handful of prepared cartridge packs and percussion caps for it.

The Yankees dragged their boat onto the shore. There was just a sliver of moon and the night was very dark, but I could make out their faint, dark shapes. I had my Enfield trained on the shadows. Then there was a brief flash of light as one of the crew sought to light their pipe with a match. The range was perhaps 700 yards, but I knew I could get him. Then I thought about what Moze had said, and I lowered my aim to the side of the launch. They all jumped as the wood splintered even before they heard the sound of musket. I didn't want to kill anybody; I just wanted them off my beach.

I quickly pulled back from my vantage and moved to the right just as two shots converged on the site where they had seen the flash of my shot. There were many sounds of excitement coming from the shore. It was hard to see, but it looked like the shore party had crouched behind the bow of their boat.

Everybody else in our group had shotguns, useless at this range, so I reloaded my Enfield.

I whispered to Robert, "Take a position about forty yards yonder," pointing to our right, then motioned to the corporal and whispered, "You go over to the other side. I'll fire and you both follow with your shotguns. We'll pepper them with shots and confuse them, make 'em think there's a lot more of us. Move after you fire or they'll know where you are."

They both ducked down and trotted over to the positions I indicated. I laid a bead with my Enfield on the shadows ahead of me and let fire another shot, again splintering the rim of the boat. Almost immediately, Robert and the corporal fired as well, then I picked up my loaded Halls and rolled several feet to the side. As I expected, someone on the shore party returned fire. The Halls didn't have the range but I aimed and fired. I heard excited exclamations and could see they were struggling with the boat. I rolled and reloaded the Enfield as I heard both of my companions fire again. There was another flash and I again took careful aim and fired. Robert fired again and then the corporal. I heard the sound of wood scraping on sand, then frantic paddling of oars. We had chased them off.

I called out to the other two, "Move back!" I was anticipating the next action. We reunited just beyond the small dunes, and we hurried a hundred yards away parallel to the water just as a flash emerged from the ship offshore, illuminating her lines quite nicely. Then there was the report of the cannon just as a shell exploded not far from where I had been firing. It was just a single shot, just to let us know who they were. It was not necessary, for we knew who they were, and now they would know who we were as well.

Twenty-two

Although it was the end of our watch, Robert and I stayed awake until light. We went down to the edge of the water where we found trace markings of where the small boat had scraped ashore. I knew Robert's shotgun had served no deadly purpose, and I reflected upon Moze's warnings about taking a life affecting my aim and felt no remorse. I had seen the pain and suffering inflicted upon men in arms and saw no need to add to the toll of war. One of them had dropped a haversack, and inside, we found tokens and remembrances that indicated our adversaries were indeed human beings with loved ones back home.

We resumed our patrol in low spirits as a cold November wind blew in our faces. When we returned to our headquarters to report, we were surprised by the news: perhaps this landing was an advance scouting party.

Captain Hale informed us, "We've received word that the Yankees have landed a force at the mouth of the Rio Grande, and they are marching along the coast, supported by gunboats."

It was assumed they were heading to retake Galveston from the land, but if so, they were coming the long way around. A force was being assembled to repel the invasion, and DeBray's cavalry would be at the core of it. Other units were joining ours, and we set in motion. We were an army six thousand strong, ready to face an invasion force of undetermined strength. Soon, we heard the union force was encamped near Indianola, and by early January, we set up along the Caney Creek to block their path. Although we suffered some bombardment over the next several weeks from the naval gunboats supporting the Yankee troops, the tension was not broken by any land action. One day, the Yankees boarded their boats and left.

"We've chased them off again," was what General Magruder said. "They didn't want any part of us."

At any rate, we returned to the north and made an encampment near Eagle Lake. But the winds of war are fickle. It became apparent to the general that this had been a feint by the Yankees, to draw our attention away from a renewed threat from the east. While we had been gathering our force to oppose a few Yankees marching up our coast, General Banks in Louisiana had been amassing a huge army to move northwest from New Orleans to take Shreveport, then swing around and lay waste to the entirety of East Texas. Magruder had been ordered to send as many men as he could to aid Generals Kirby Smith and Richard Taylor in Louisiana.

As the rumors were flying, we noticed the Twenty-sixth was not in any way preparing for travel. We soldiers were alarmed at our inactivity because most were itching for a real fight. We surmised General Magruder wanted us to stay to protect Texas from any surprise attack from the sea. Colonel DeBray could not stomach this, and he pressed the issue with General Magruder.

Then we finally received the order we had been wishing for: we were to pack up and move out. On March 14, we hastened to break camp and move on to Houston where we could make final preparations by tending to our horses and gathering supplies. Prize was shoed for the journey. As news of this activity spread, Pa steamed up the Buffalo Bayou to see me. We had a very emotional departure, for it was obvious to everyone the Twenty-sixth was heading out for some real action and we expected a protracted campaign.

On March 17, we left Houston with perhaps four hundred and fifty active cavalry along with a train of thirty-two wagons. Colonel DeBray, who had left the command of our unit to Colonel Myers so he could attend to his duties as the commander of the sub-district of Houston, resumed full command of the brigade for this march. Colonel Myers was left to organize the remainder of our troops, mostly the sick and furloughed. They would serve as a reserve when they rejoined us.

We were hampered by our long supply train, but we marched in good order as we were trained to do. Over the next many days, we slowly made our way north and east. Our first objective was supposed to be Alexandria in Louisiana.

Captain Hare gave us the bad news. "Alexandria has fallen, boys, so our new objective is a place called Mansfield."

Mansfield is somewhat south and east of Shreveport. Our path toward the Louisiana border was blocked by several swollen streams, and our progress was slowed by the meager means we had to effect passage across them, namely small and slow private ferry services.

By April 1, we were at the Sabine and were happy to find a very nice ferry operated there. Our entire force was quickly assembled on the other side of the river. That night, we camped near a town called Many, Louisiana, about twenty miles into the state.

"This is the first time I've ever been out of Texas," Rufus informed me.

We left the next morning in fine form, and a lone confederate officer in uniform rode past us. We later learned he had praised our form to the colonel and seemed quite surprised to find out such a fine outfit as ours had come from Texas. Not far from Many, we received orders to change our destination to a position to the east of Many, so we had to countermarch a ways. It was reported there were Federals who might seek to flank our army.

We were to reinforce Bagby's unit near an old fort called Jessup. We had not marched very far before we heard artillery fire and then the crack of muskets, and we steadied ourselves for a conflict. We did not have long to wait.

Our advance scouts encountered Federal cavalry, and it became apparent those fellows were between us and Bagby. Soon the far away firing seemed to die down, but then it renewed much closer as the Yankees began fighting us in earnest. Couriers from Bagby arrived by a round-about route and informed us they had fallen back because they were out of ammunition. We began a delayed withdrawal ourselves. We had suffered a few wounded, and I was gratified to see our regimental band, who had gone to the rear and dismounted, had taken it upon themselves to take the field and evacuate our wounded. Very shortly, the Yankees broke off the fight.

Although we had shown them some strength, Captain Hare suspected it was just a delaying tactic on their parts.

"I presume they suspected we were the vanguard of a superior force."

We rejoined Bagby and hastened our march to a place called Pleasant Hill.

When we arrived at Pleasant Hill, we heard General Taylor was agitated at the tardiness of our arrival. Colonel DeBray was quite offended and explained the length of our march and the cause of our many delays, including the skirmish at Fort Jessup.

I assume things were patched up fine and good since we soon occupied the field and posted pickets at that spot. I took my turn like the rest, and the night passed slowly. I am sure the uncertainty of not knowing when or where our Yankee counterparts might try to ruin our day only added to the tedium. Because of the threat, we kept our mounts at the ready, and the horses were quite agitated by this turn of affair as they enjoyed their time out of the saddle.

April 3 was a quiet day. We knew the Yankees were on the move, but General Taylor ordered the infantry at Pleasant Hill to march to Mansfield. We were left at Pleasant Hill along with Bagby's brigade and Vincent's Louisiana Cavalry.

"I wish somebody would do something. This waiting wears on my nerves," Robert White said to me.

"Be careful what you wish for," I replied.

There was no action April 4 except for short patrols and continued picket duty. The next day, we encountered patrolling union cavalry and harassed them as best as we could but were ordered to simply delay them and fall back. Fighting these rear actions slowed our progress as we made our way to rejoin our main force at Mansfield twenty-five miles away.

According to rumor, General Taylor was under orders to not engage the enemy. Kirby Smith endeavored to deliver a crushing blow further north, but Taylor had determined the Federals had made a mistake in their march. They were coming right down one main road when there were alternate roads available they could have used to diffuse their forces and protect them from possible annihilation. This was, even we lowly cavalrymen knew, standard military protocol.

"General Banks is a politician, not a soldier," we were told. "Which is good for us because he is prone to make mistakes like this."

By April 7, we had joined General Taylor's forces, and we were held in the reserve on the far right of his line. He was planning to block Banks' advance at that point, despite Kirby's wishes. We relished the chance to refresh our supplies and ammunition because our provisions had suffered due to our delaying actions. With so many infantry about, ammunition for my Enfield was plentiful, so I grabbed as much as I could carry.

Picket fire was sporadic throughout the night of the seventh. Everyone knew a major battle was likely coming the next day, and each and every one of us felt we were ready. Our skirmish outside the town of Many, along with our brief flare-ups at Pleasant Hill and on the road to Mansfield, had proven we were a force to be reckoned with.

"Jack, are you afraid of what might happen tomorrow?"

"Naw. Just remember your training and stay close, Rufus."

For most of us, our thoughts were with our families. I must confess I did think of my pa and wondered if my sweet mother was watching down from heaven. I heard many a man and boy praying through the night, some praying they would be spared, and some praying they would not let their comrades down. Many a soldier placed a note in their pocket with their name and the location of their family.

Instead of praying, for some reason I thought of my trick bag and pulled it out of my pocket. I had last put it in the light of a full moon in March, while we were still in Texas, dutifully placing it in the fork of a nearby tree as Vanita had instructed. It was a dark night, just past the new moon. Rufus had fallen asleep praying and was snoring nearby. Suddenly he was gasping for breath, soundlessly mouthing words in his sleep, and he seemed in quite a bit of distress. I shook him and called his name, and finally he snapped out of it. He was drenched in sweat.

"Jack! Jack!"

"Shhhh. Take a deep breath, Rufus," I said. "You had a nightmare."

"I couldn't breathe, I, I, I..." he was gulping air.

"It's just worry. We're facing the Yankees tomorrow. I'm worried, too."

"That's not it. There was a voice in my ear, like someone was sitting on my chest and whispering to me."

I was startled by this news, but I kept trying to reassure him even though I had a very cold feeling sweep through me.

"I was whispering for you to wake up."

"No, it was something else," he said and he sat up and rummaged through a bag with his belongings. He pulled out a long leather thong.

"Here, I was told to give you this," he said. "Tie it around the red bag you keep secret, then secure it around your neck."

"Wh...what red bag?"

"We all know about it. We've seen you hiding it and trying to keep it out of sight. She told me to tell you this."

"Who?"

"I don't know who. It was in my dream, but it was real, clear as day."

"Did you hear a name? Can you remember?"

"I, I, I... wait... Vanita, that was the name. She told me to tell you this. What does it mean, Jack?"

I was finally able to calm Rufus down and get him to go back to a fitful sleep, but I didn't sleep the rest of the night. The first thing I did was take his leather thong and do as he instructed. I tied the trick-bag to the thong, slipped it over my head, and buried it under my red flannel shirt. Then I sat and pondered this event the rest of the night.

"Vanita," I whispered to myself.

Twenty-three

When one thinks of a battle, the images conjured in a general person's mind are two masses of soldiers facing each other as a single unit, fighting it out face to face in a personal and enduring conflict. It is not like that at all. As the Yankee Army came into the area of Mansfield, although their numbers were superior to ours, General Taylor had arranged for us to meet them with sufficient strength to give them a good fight. The Twenty-sixth was set as a reserve on the far right of our lines.

We had been in a few skirmishes and scrapes in the recent past, but these experiences did not keep our hearts from racing as we prepared ourselves to face a real battle. The fact we were being held back distressed us because many of us were spoiling for a fight. When the thing started, we were shocked, because you cannot imagine the noise of it all.

First, the artillery begins to boom in a succession of explosions on both sides, then the rhythm is broken into piecemeal firing as each gun crew works amid the dust, smoke, and sweat to reload and fire again and again.

Then there comes a volley of muskets, as the infantry fires in unison. This routine repeats for one or two volleys, and then all decorum breaks loose as the soldiers, each and every one on both sides, begin firing just as fast as they can. The crescendo moves like the flow of a river, with eddies and whirlpools of action moving up and down the line, occasionally broken apart as troops maneuver and the artillery on both sides tries to reposition to gain better vantage on the distant enemy.

Through it all, amid the smoke, comes the sound of hooves and neighs, along with the rattling of caissons and heavy gun carriages. Amid the continuous crash of artillery and musket, you hear the sounds of the wounded and dying, crying in pain or anguish. An ever-present sobbing permeates this din, as soldiers call out for their dear mothers to come take them away from this Satan's inferno of existence. Best friends lie dead or dying in each other's arms and their comrades ignore them because they cannot give up the fight lest they, too, fall prey to a piece of hot lead. To witness even a tiny portion of this is to take a brief glimpse into what hell must surely be like.

To be in the thick of it must be bad enough, but to be set to the side, immobile, listening, watching, and waiting, is surely the most helpless feeling in the world. Those of us held in reserve began to question the sanity of our generals using us like some lost pawns on a forgotten chessboard.

Rufus called out to me, "Why don't they send us in?"

I shook my head. "I don't know."

But before I could continue my answer, the lieutenant came riding to us, calling out, "No talking, keep our line straight, remember this is DeBray's Brigade! Stand ready!"

We held the reins tight on our fidgety mounts and stared into the maelstrom, or what we could see of it through the smoky haze, and fought against the fingers of fear massaging our insides.

Prize stood fast, but many other horses were unsure of the horror around us and were quite hard to control. Quiet words were heard up and down the line as the soldiers leaned forward and lied, telling their mounts, "Everything's going to be all right."

I reckoned Prize had seen her share of action and knew that, come what may, she'd treat me with the same duty and loyalty she had given her previous rider. Though he was shot off her, she had stayed close by the spot, loyal to the end.

I searched somewhere in my memory, trying to find Moze's kindly old face, his white whiskers peppering his chin, hoping his visage would give me some of his ancient wisdom, but I could find nothing. Truth be told, he never wanted to be part of a fight, and I knew he had tried his best to keep me out of this one.

I touched my breast where the trick bag was hanging by the leather thong Rufus had given me. I, of course, knew he had fallen victim to the hag-rider Vanita, sending a renewed message of protection. I hoped against hope her magic was real and it would stick with me through the coming fury. I wondered why she hadn't ridden me, but realized she no doubt encouraged Rufus to keep watch over me as well. I looked up and down our line, wondering if perhaps she had similarly touched others.

In the waning hours of the afternoon, when it appeared the Yankees were falling back, we were given the order to advance. We moved forward in our typical fine form and attacked the enemy. They were in disarray, but they still managed to turn, re-form, and make a good show of force against us. I did not have a saber like our officers, so I lifted my carbine and others lifted their shotguns and revolvers. I could not shoot effectively at full gallop, but I did fire several times at nothing in particular. I managed to drop several cartridges as I attempted to reload while the horse was on the run. Even in retreat, they were not afraid to give us a good fight. We returned to our lines, a bit bruised and battered, with some of our men still on the field, gallant corpses to the cause.

We were ordered to turn and slowly pursue and harass them.

Sergeant Murphy had suffered a wound in his arm, but it was bandaged and he was back in the saddle, urging us forward. "We need to keep up with them to help General Taylor anticipate their next moves."

They fell back several miles to the southeast and stopped at a place called Pleasant Hill, the same place where we had camped for several days previous to this battle. We had already skirmished with the Yankees there and were familiar with the terrain. We held our position and kept guard while the rest of our army followed.

Moving an army quickly is difficult because it is not just the men that need to move. Supply trains must follow, for they have the food, medical supplies, and ammunition. After hearing the sounds of the previous day's battle, I could not imagine we still had a single barrel of powder left, but we all replenished our supplies as best as we could. The Twenty-sixth stood watch through the night and a good deal of the next day. Both armies were waiting with great anticipation. As the battle lines were drawn up, we once again found ourselves held in reserve.

"Saving the best for the last again," Robert White remarked.

But we were under the watchful eyes of our sergeants and officers, so we kept such chatter to a minimum. It was no matter, as each and every one of us preferred to be alone with our own thoughts and prayers. My carbine was at the ready. The battle seemed more haphazard today, but the sound was just as ferocious, like a pack of roaring lions pacing up and down the line. When the order came, we were at the ready and moved forward then out into the field, galloping and yelling like a throng of banshees.

Unlike the day before, we rode into a veritable field of death. Unbeknownst to us, a crowd of Yankees had found a position protected by a thick stand of young pines. Their good cover was further enhanced by a deep gully where they could fire at us from ground level. We first became aware of them as we charged when a volley of musket fire tore our long-practiced lines apart.

I saw a trooper fall near me and, without thinking, I dropped off Prize and ran to the prone figure. I was dismayed to see it was my old friend, Ricardo Zavala.

"Ricky, are you okay?" I knew it was a useless comment because I could see the huge hole torn into his shirt by a Minié ball with bright red, warm blood oozing out in a pool underneath.

"Jack," he whispered to me. "Jack, I fear I am killed. Tell my mother my last thoughts are of her."

His body went limp, and I knew he was dead. I didn't have time to dwell on it as Rufus rode back to me.

"Jack, leave him be, we *must* keep moving!"

I remounted, and Rufus rode ahead, keeping his mount between me and the deadly stand of trees.

"Stay behind me, Jack!"

We tried to push on, but our charge had fallen into disarray. Our casualties were great, but we continued taking the battle to the Yankees. I saw Captain Hare fall, yet we continued moving, firing at the Yankees with great abandon. I admit, shocked at my friend's death, at that moment, I wanted to kill the attackers despite what Moze had told me. I fired into the line once, but I was out of ammunition afterward. In the excitement, I forgot about my revolver.

At what seemed like the height of the battle, I felt something huge slam into my chest with a dull thud, and I was knocked out of my saddle. I fell flat on my back and experienced the unusual feeling of having the wind knocked out of me twice in quick succession. I'd fallen out of the saddle before, but this was more than that.

Moze came into my thoughts, and I had a mental image of him calmly talking to me, reminding me, *"Relax them lungs, don't try to force no breath none."*

Then for a brief moment I panicked, afraid I was shot and wondering if I was dying.

I remember thinking to myself, "I don't want to be a martyr to a lost cause."

But the image of Moze returned and kept counsel with me, telling me to relax, and then I remembered something he said to me after one bad fall off of Elvira.

"Raise up your arms over your haid."

When I did this, I imagined something strange, the image of an angel seemed to be blowing the tiniest puff of air into my lungs, allowing them to release their grip. I could breathe again, although it was shallow at first.

As I regained my composure, I was aware of a pronounced pain in my chest. I reached up expecting to feel warm and sticky blood but felt instead the trick-bag. I became aware of something warm on my belly, between my shirt and my skin. I felt around and found the hot lump of a partially deformed Minié ball.

Prize had stopped when I fell, and she returned and began to nudge me with her snout. At almost the same time, Rufus rode up to me and dismounted at a run. He knelt by my side, out of breath.

"Jack, Jack, are you kilt?"

I shook my head, "I don't think so. Wind knocked out of me."

I slowly got up with Rufus' help. I raised my small discovery. "Look at this," I said.

"Musta been spent. If you're okay, we better get back in the saddle and get out of here."

A bugle call went down the line telling us to pull back, so we mounted and rejoined a part of the Twenty-sixth along with stragglers from other units and moved back, still under fire from those hidden Yankees. Back under the cover of some woods to our rear, I dismounted again and Robert White embraced me.

"I saw you fall, Jack, are you all right?" Then he looked down at my chest. "I see red... should we call the surgeon?"

I felt my chest but it was dry, then found the hole in my shirt. My trick-bag was right behind the hole. I unclasped the button and showed the bag. "You just saw this... the red bag."

"That good luck charm of yours!" he exclaimed. "Darn near gave me a fit."

For the first time since I had acquired it, I opened the bag and looked inside and saw that one of the trinkets inside had been a piece of lodestone. I had surmised one good-sized object I had felt inside it was some kind of rock, but now instead of one, there were three smaller stones inside.

"Don't have a fit about my good luck charm, but I think it saved my life," I said.

Rufus came up and dismounted and then looked at me and correctly surmised the situation. He blinked at me in disbelief. He gasped, "Your bag... it stopped the Minié ball?"

"I guess it did at that. Rufus, you saved me." I replaced the contents, along with the flattened projectile, tied the bag shut, and put it back around my neck.

He looked at me with his mouth open, like I was magic or something, but this spell was interrupted by a lieutenant riding up.

"You men, fall back in line. Benson, are you injured?"

"Just a spent round, sir. It knocked me off my horse."

"Do you need the surgeon?"

I shook my head. "I'll be fine, sir."

"Thank the Lord; he's already got his hands full."

We were ordered to dismount and support Walker's infantry who had taken up the fight. The Federals were quickly pushed out of the stand of trees where their fire had decimated our ranks. The battlefield shortly fell into an uneasy calm, with only intermittent pops of musket fire.

The Twenty-sixth regrouped and were placed on picket duty along with some other cavalry units, primarily Bushel. The rest of our army, finding little to no fresh water near our position, endeavored to fall back several miles to a small stream.

We, the chosen few, kept watch over the battlefield while our dead and wounded were gathered. I had a huge bruise on my chest, but I was otherwise unmolested by the battle. There was occasional fire from both sides all night. Word came along the line that Major Menard had been seriously wounded. Captain Hare was in bad shape as well, but both of them had been luckier than Captain Peck of Company F. He along with Ricardo and quite a number of our men had been killed. Colonel DeBray himself had his horse shot out from under him and had injured his leg in the process, but he was still in command.

Things seemed quiet over toward Pleasant Hill, and around daybreak, a reconnaissance patrol from one of the other companies set out to find the Yankees. We assumed they would renew the attack at the earliest opportunity, but the word came back that the enemy had withdrawn in the night. We later heard the Yankees would call this battle a Union victory, but those of us who lived it considered it a draw at best. In the Twenty-sixth, we knew we were in possession of the field at daybreak.

We had scant time to rest. The purpose of cavalry was to pursue, and our scouts reported Butler appeared to be withdrawing to Grande Ecore. We assumed this was so he could board boats and skedaddle back down the Red River.

Those past two days had brought us to the reason for our existence. Those who say there is glory in battle have not experienced the full brunt of the experience. I will admit there is exhilaration. A person's heart starts to pounding to the point where his head will start asking, "Am I up to the task?" To ride into a hail of bullets is a frightful thing indeed, but when you are part of an army, you fully realize that these fellows you've joked and eaten with for several years past are your brothers. Our presence alongside each other serves to help us spur each other on even as we spur our horses on. The presence of these men serves to take the fear from your mind and spread it out into a conglomerate of courage.

Fear? Yes, there is a fear of bullet and shell, a fear of showing cowardice in the face of one's brothers, and a fear of death, but through it all, one finds solace in the realization that all of your comrades share these same feelings. Emboldened by these deliberations, there is no other thought but to embrace the enemy and continue forward into the face of an uncertain future. In later days, there may come a notion of glory, but at the time, there is no thought of it. It is a matter of survival, both of you and your brothers.

We expected a resumption of the attack, but as is common in the army, things do not progress in the same ways we lowly soldiers think they should. We heard rumors General Kirby Smith was not pleased with the results we had achieved. He had ordered our armies to slowly withdraw up to Shreveport where he had another body of troops waiting for Butler. Taylor had been ordered not to engage. The fact that Butler had been turned back seemed not important.

But we were simple privates. The way we saw it, we had a chance to deliver a crushing blow to the Yankees. Of course, we still did not quite fathom the fact that the Yankees vastly outnumbered us, and as they withdrew to the river again, they had the protection of the larger naval artillery. Taylor was still ordered to send the larger part of his force to rejoin Kirby to go pursue other actions in Arkansas. The cavalry would remain behind and harass the retreating Yankees wherever possible.

Sergeant Murphy gave us our orders. "Mount up, boys, we're headed to a place called Monnett's Bluff on the Cane River."

The bluecoats peppered us regularly with artillery fire, which is a dreadful thing to endure. Then they attacked us. In truth, it was nothing more than a skirmish, but we endured two assaults and withdrew on the third to better preserve ourselves for another day. Our primary orders were to attack and annoy, and we did it by night marches and skirmishes, always alerting the Yankees to our presence, which kept them moving steadily away.

To this end, we made a night march to Beasley's Station and then to McNutt's Hill, all locations that would barely catch a traveler's notice on a journey, but I remember them because to us they were places we encountered and skirmished with Yankee infantry or cavalry. Around this time, we were reinforced with the sick and furloughed men Colonel Myers had stayed behind to organize. He had found us with some difficulty because of our circuitous movements, but the reunion with these friends was a welcome relief to our tired and depleted forces.

As Butler moved across Louisiana, he made the state suffer for his trouble. Alexandria was torched, but by rapid movement of our forces, including the Twenty-sixth, the town of Marksville was saved from a similar fate. Butler was forced to detour by our presence. Still, there was plenty of action. At Mansura Prairie, there was a grand artillery duel of some duration, which created a lot of smoke and noise but not much else. There was no general engagement, simply a show of force that was impressive to hear from a distance.

From our squad, Bill Teal, who served primarily as a bugler, was captured in late April. Such were the fortunes of war. I wondered at his fate and how it might compare to mine the previous year. Rumors informed us that exchanges had stopped, and then we heard more rumors of frightful conditions in Yankee prisons. I'm sure it was no better on our side, because the deprivations of war were so much greater in the South.

We proceeded like this for several weeks. Finally, as Butler's army prepared to cross the Atchafalaya, we attacked their rear, and they tired of our annoyance and turned to face us. Although I'm sure it was simply a mere skirmish in general terms, we suffered many casualties there. This attack near Norwood Plantation gained us nothing. While we regrouped and counted our losses, they crossed the Atchafalaya, just as they had always intended, and in fact, this was what we wanted them to do anyway. They had pontoon bridges to facilitate their crossing, but we had none, so we could not pursue them beyond that point. This was in mid-May. Our involvement with what is now called The Red River Campaign was over.

Twenty-four

There was some fear of a renewed Union effort to move up into Louisiana, and our forces were divided, some taking up duty along the Atchafalaya, which is a river full of huge swampy areas with tiny settlements sprinkled throughout the region like islands. The rest of our forces were on the move, maintaining general order and giving the overall impression that we meant to maintain control of the rest of Louisiana. In July, we had a nice surprise when Bill Teal returned to our camp, exchanged by the Yankees. For us, it was another false rumor put to rest.

"They treated me poorly," he said. "I was starving most of the time and always on the move. I hear tell there aren't any exchanges in the east, but here, Butler just didn't want to be bothered with prisoners."

The swamp duty was considered a difficult task, and thus it was rotated among the various commands. Throughout the summer and early autumn, Company K moved about, spending time in Opelousas, Alexandria, and Natchitoches. In October, it came time for our duty along the river, and we dutifully took up our post, spreading patrols throughout the swampy areas.

This service took a toll on our horses because of the limited amount of fodder. It also took a toll on our men as our supplies had seriously dwindled or deteriorated in the constant wetness of the swamps. Our clothing suffered as well, and some men came down with malarial fever. As a whole, our men were constantly miserable and hungry. Eventually, many began to suffer from dysentery as well because it was difficult to maintain good sanitary practices. We lacked medicine for this but substituted a salty vinegar solution that sometimes helped.

I still had my captured Enfield, and after the previous battles, I had scrounged a considerable amount of ammunition for it because every downed Federal soldier had percussion caps and prepared paper cartridges. Thus, I was able to use my skill with the rifle to augment our meager supplies with fresh meat.

I wondered what old Jeff Davis might have said if he knew the lessons of an old slave named Moze were keeping soldiers alive out in this dismal swamp. Whatever his thoughts, my training served me well, and I amazed my comrades with my skills. We primarily feasted on gator because they were the most plentiful, but I would occasionally bag a buck or some game birds. A good-sized gator could feed my entire squad for several days and would sometimes feed some of those on duty to either side of us.

I'd hunt early in the morning, as Moze had taught me, watching for a tell-tale swish from under the water as one of the big beasts was slowly stalking something, possibly me, moving itself along by flipping its big tail. I knew they would periodically poke their snout and eyes above the surface, and I'd be ready, Enfield loaded, primed and cocked. No one but me had eaten alligator in my squad, and at first, most declined the notion. Once the aroma of the cooking meat permeated the area, though, it generally brought everyone to the table.

One day, I was stalking a huge bull alligator as he swam along. I fired my Enfield and thought I had hit it directly on his head, but for some reason, the shot did not dispatch the beast. It appeared I had only made him mad. He immediately located the source of his pain and determined to exact revenge. With a flick of his tail, he came to the shoreline and lunged up at me as I scampered away from him, fumbling for my Colt. He snapped viciously at me, all the while moving forward until I fired two shots into his skull with him not two feet away.

The Enfield was accurate but was too powerful for most small game. I'd borrow one of the boys' shotguns to do my duty on smaller game. It being fall, we had our pick of duck and goose. These weren't gaming guns, but I could lay a bead on a flock of ducks and usually bring down several when they took to the air.

~ * ~

The deprivations of swamp duty pushed many in the Twenty-sixth to abandon the decorum of their good discipline. Rumors of theft from remote cabins and families reached our ears, and the assumption was that our brother soldiers were starving and taking what food they could in order to survive. Beef and chicken were among the most prized thefts. I repeatedly asked the sergeant to allow me to go meet with other squads and teach them to feed themselves. These swamps seem inhospitable to folks unused to the conditions, but Moze had taught me they were a paradise of game.

"You just stay here and do your duty, Jack."

I don't think he wanted to be deprived of my services in this regard, and anyway, the entire brigade was stretched over a large area. It was not practical for me to head off into the unknown. When we had extra meat, we did pass it along down the line.

I managed a few barters with some locals, trading fresh meat for fish hooks, and I set lines across small bodies of water, baited with gator entrails. Nearly every morning, we pulled a bounty of fish out of the swamp. We shared this as well. I foraged for wild onions and other roots Moze had taught me to spot in the swamplands near Houston.

One day on patrol with Rufus, Bill Teal, and Adam Huffman, we happened upon a small group of Negroes. I had spied something in the distance and, thinking we might add venison to our table, had instead tracked down this small group. I suppose it was a family. They were mighty afraid and very hungry.

"Must be escaped slaves," Adam said.

"Maybe," I agreed.

"Should we take them back and turn them in?" Rufus asked.

I shook my head. "Those aren't our orders. Leave them be."

"But if they're escaped—" Bill started.

"Leave them be," I repeated.

I knew the others subscribed to the old notion of property, assuming that every member of the black race was tied to some form of servitude. It was all they knew. I chose a different course; we had our own situation and should not be bothered with any old ideas.

The leader of the group spoke, "Suh, we ain't meaning to be no trouble. The Sappaneux plantation where we lived was raided by those bluecoats a while back, and they run all the white folks off afore they burned the place. We wuz told we wuz free, but well, they went on and we wuz alone and didn't know where to go, so we been prowling this here swamp, ketchin' what foods we can. We ain't no bother to no one, I just trying to keep my family alive."

Black faces and the whites of wide eyes stared back at us.

"We need to take them and turn them in," Rufus said.

"To who?" I was sternly staring at Rufus. "You seen a sheriff in the last few weeks?"

He shook his head then dropped his chin. I think he realized he was trying to adhere to a notion that just didn't seem right anymore.

"Leave them be," I again intoned.

"Suh," the Negro said, "we are powerful hungry. I been hearing a flock of wild turkey out yonder," he pointed. "Been trying to snare us one, but wit' them shotguns, we might grab the whole flock. I'll show you where they are congregating if you can share some o' the meat with us."

I handed my Enfield to Bill, and he gave me his shotgun. I told the man, "Show me where."

Rufus and Bill stayed with the others while Adam and I followed the man along a path through the overgrowth to a spot about a half mile away. He put his finger to his mouth and we crept along. I could hear the big birds softly chattering to themselves. Using a trick Moze had taught me, I gently made a rhythmic clicking sound with my tongue, not so loud as to alarm the birds but enough to hopefully get their curiosity up.

Turkeys are both curious and stupid. I had earlier instructed Adam to raise his shotgun when I raised mine, and we both aimed at the grove of bushes where we were hearing the sounds. I clicked again, and three heads popped above the leaves. Twin explosions erupted from our guns, and after a moment's hesitation, feathers flew amidst a panic of birds in a desperate attempt to get away. I fired again with the other barrel. The smoke cleared as the echoes died away and the woods were quiet again. The Negro ran to the clump of bushes.

"Woo-hee!" he exclaimed, and he reached down and lifted three dead birds by their necks. A fourth, hit on the fly, was a few yards away. They were all of good size.

Adam stayed back at our vantage post while I surveyed the scene of the massacre, looking to see if there was more good meat to be found. The Negro caught my arm and whispered, "Is you Captain Jack?"

"Huh?" I said, taken unawares.

"My missus was done hag-ridden last night, and she said da hag done tole her to not be afeared 'cause a white man named Captain Jack was gonna give us some help."

I was a bit shaken by this sudden revelation, but I nodded.

"Don't say anything about this to the others."

He gave me a brief nod, and we gathered up two more birds we found in the bushes.

When we returned to his camp, I gave him two of the birds, and we took the others and continued our patrol.

"Thank you, suh," he said.

Our squad feasted on the turkey that night. The other boys said nothing of our encounter. I think they were conflicted by my insistence we not turn the runaways in.

Our swamp duty continued throughout October and November. Toward the end of November, our hellish tour ended just as a chill blue 'norther pushed through. We assembled and bundled up as best as we could and followed our new orders with elation. We were headed back home to Texas!

Twenty-five

Never in my army service had I felt such a feeling of relief as I did when we departed the ferry crossing at the Sabine River and I entered Texas again. Other soldiers felt the same, and I actually saw a few dismount and kiss the soil. Our first camp was at Sabinetown on the other side of the river. Our supplies were so depleted at this point the quartermasters endeavored to feed us by using the stipulations of the Impressment Act. The army declared our need and seized what we needed from local communities. To this end, we followed a circuitous route, first through San Augustin, then we proceeded north where we encamped at Carthage. Low morale depleted our ranks, but we continued as best as we could.

From Carthage, we moved to a camp at Henderson. The region had scant supplies, but we fed ourselves as best as we could and tried not to overly burden the populace with our needs. Finally, we headed back south toward the region around Crockett, and we rode out a couple of winter storms there. My musket provided many a side of venison for our larder, courtesy of the forests of East Texas.

In March, we finally moved into a camp near Richmond at a small place called Pittsville. This was near Walker's infantry division. The supplies near Houston were more substantial, but we, every one of us, was suffering from the scant provisions we were given. The news from the east was a further depression on the minds of the men. Slowly but surely, some men began to wander away from their service. Rufus endeavored to be one of those. He confided to me one night as we were moving south toward Houston that he very much missed his mother.

"Jack, this war is over," he said. "I miss my mother something fierce. I need to just break away and go home, just to make sure she's all right."

"We signed up for the misery and hardship as much as for the glory," I reminded him. "I ain't seen my pa for just as long. It is our duty to stay here."

He just shook his head, "No, Jack, my ma is old, and I know the war has been as much a hardship for her as it has been for us. More, maybe. I need to just see if she is well."

One dark night as we were marching south, Rufus wheeled his horse off the road into some underbrush and disappeared. I wondered if he might have asked for a furlough, but the rumor going around the brigade was that furloughs were suspended.

Captain Hare had returned from the hospital, not fully healed from his wounds, and was obviously still in some distress as he rode. Unit organization had suffered in the wake of our hardships, but for those of us who had remained in the saddle, our overall discipline was still good. Our years of training continued to guide most of us.

I wished Rufus well and hoped he would not be arrested as a deserter. He was not the only soldier entertaining notions of home at this stage of the war. I only had my pa to worry about, and he was a man who tended to his own business so I knew he was okay in my absence. Beyond him, with Moze gone, civilian life was more of a question mark in my life than my current condition, so I held fast to my honor and my duty.

We had once been a proud brigade, and I presumed we still were, but the overwhelming weight of bad news we heard did little for morale. In days past, the bond of our comradeship would seemingly get us through the toughest times. Because our squad had not starved on our duty in the swamp, I think we still felt good about our ability to continue the war as long as our country needed us, but I could not say the same about the members of other companies.

~ * ~

A dark cloud hung over the brigade in these days. Our proximity to Houston meant we got more timely news of the far-away events, and none of the news was good. General Johnston had given a strong show of force in North Carolina against General Sherman, who had captured Atlanta then cut a swath of destruction across Georgia. But an army needs more than food and ammunition to fight. It needs a sustained will to fight, and the light of that ideal seemed to be dimming a little more every day. New information reached us: Johnston was defeated and Sherman had pushed on to Raleigh. Most in our ranks knew the end was near.

The siege at Petersburg was also a continued source of concern. By all accounts, Lee's army was dwindling day by day and, as the weather warmed, the resolve of General Grant was growing. The Union was warming up to the notion of putting Lee's army to the final test. Soon, it was assumed, Sherman would meet up with Grant, and then we all knew the war in the east would be over. How these events might affect us in the west was anybody's guess.

There was a widely held notion that Texas would forever be independent like we were after San Jacinto.

Robert White spoke to me about this one day. "Despite our losses, the Twenty-sixth is still formidable. Maybe we could just become part of the army in the New Republic of Texas."

He was not alone. This notion emboldened many.

But I didn't agree. "The South has cost the Union a lot in terms of men and money. I doubt they'll be satisfied to let us do that. It might mean the destruction of us all."

It was a sobering thought, but after having seen the wealth and power of the North, I knew they were not about to relinquish any part of their perceived victory.

Then I added, "Besides, Texas failed as a republic. Isn't that why we joined up with the United States in the first place? How could such a thing come out of the ashes of this destructive war?"

The citizenry, we knew, was despondent at the notion of continued conflict. Our impressment of supplies had eroded even the slightest notion of duty and responsibility to either the Confederate States of America or to Texas. People, by and large, just wanted to end their misery and go on living.

I thought back to the family of former slaves I met in the swamps of the Atchafalaya and realized they were no different. All that father had wanted was some meat to keep his family alive, and I was glad to give it to him. This was why I had admonished my comrades when they mentioned turning them in as runaways. They were just hungry people, same as us.

Robert rushed to me with more news. "Petersburg and Richmond have fallen! Jeff Davis is on the run, but General Lee is still trying to maintain a rear action against Grant's army."

Then word reached us in April that a meeting had taken place at a tiny spot in Virginia called Appomattox Court House. Most of us imagined an impressive stone building of some stature, but Captain Hare told us the truth.

"Generals Lee and Grant met in the parlor of a house. Lee surrendered the Army of Northern Virginia."

Because of Lee's stature and almost mythic reputation, this carried a lot of weight in the collective minds of military men everywhere in the Confederate States. Other armies had been surrendered over the years with no more notice than for one to say, "so-and-so at such-and-such a place has surrendered," and life would go on. But this time, once General Lee had fallen, those notions changed. It was like a jug had been cracked and all the liquid was flowing out of it unabated. Our resolve to continue the war leaked out like the fluid in the cracked jug. There seemed to be no more point to it all.

Still, as far as we knew, we in the west were still at war, and I was still in the cavalry. The Twenty-sixth moved our camp again to a spot outside Hempstead. We had been there but a few days when General DeBray—for he had been promoted to Brigadier General after Pleasant Hill—called us together and told us we were going to return to Houston.

"Local government functions have broken down to the point where lawlessness is taking hold," he said.

Houston had become the major supply and business center of Texas during the war. Other commanders were going to take their commands to other places like Austin and San Antonio, but since we were recruited in Houston, we would return home in an effort to maintain order. We arrived in Houston just as the news of Lincoln's death reached the city, and this news only enhanced a great fear of continued lawlessness. The culprits of these actions were rogue vagabonds, mostly deserters. The presence of armed cavalry did much to calm the city. We dealt harshly with any lawlessness, and soon many such scalawags departed the area.

The widow Jenkins saw me riding along the street one day and motioned to me.

"Jack, it is so good to see you. Do you know, will this war go much longer?"

"I don't rightly know, Mrs. Jenkins, but I suspect it is pretty much over."

"What will you do then?"

I shook my head, "I don't know, ma'am, I don't know."

"I was wondering if you'd come back to my place. I need to get my garden planted again, and I have suffered to keep my house in one piece without you and Moze. I couldn't pay you but could give you a warm place to sleep and, with your help, could put some food on the table."

"That's a generous offer, Mrs. Jenkins. I'll look you up when I am able."

"Thank you, Jack."

I rode off, content with the knowledge I had a place to go when the inevitable happened.

Within a few days, we were all assembled where we had made our camp. Houston had become much more manageable with our strong show of force, but food and ammunition were diminished to critical levels, and with the Confederate government basically gone, we had no means of procuring supplies. General DeBray concluded along with his staff that the time had come to disband the unit.

"I know your service has been long and hard, but you have served admirably. Take the discipline and order we have instilled in you and apply it to your daily lives and you will do well. I promise you that."

Afterward, we ceremoniously folded our banners and flags, and there were many tears, handshakes, and even manly embraces. As we were saying our goodbyes at camp, one of the men in another company spoke of William Shakespeare's play *Henry V*, where a soldier's life was referred to as a band of brothers. It seemed fitting.

We had lived together, served together, and some of us had even died, all for a country that no longer existed. We, each and every one of us, swore to do just what General DeBray urged us to do: take what we had learned of discipline and order and apply it to our continued daily lives. He told us he was proud of our service, and to tell the truth, in spite of my reservations about the futility of it all, so was I. For each of us, it was the beginning of a new chapter in our lives.

I was on my way home from our camp, walking Prize through a deserted and dense thicket, when I was accosted by a ruffian, the type of fellow we had been chasing out of Houston. He was holding a Bowie knife and had a distinct tinge of desperation in his voice.

"Hand over the horse and all your bags and guns," he said.

I took a step toward him. His dirty tunic showed butternut and grey beneath a layer of grime.

He motioned with his knife. "Stop right there."

"I'm just a homeless soldier, just like you."

"No matter, hand everything over."

There had been a chill in the air, a rare May occurrence in the Houston area, so I had draped the remnants of my blanket over my shoulders. I reasoned it was concealing the fully loaded Colt revolver stuck in my belt. As I faced the man, I wondered if I might be able to grab it and cock it before the massive knife found my heart. I brushed my hand down and began to panic when I realized it was gone.

"Keep your hands where I can see them. I ain't gonna have to kill you, am I?"

Then a voice I had not heard in two long years punctuated the conversation.

"You ain't going to do any such thing!"

The man's eyes widened in surprise, and as he began to turn with his knife raised, an explosion rang out and he crumpled into a heap at my feet. Through the haze of smoke, I saw a small grey-haired figure with a cloudy eye holding my Colt revolver.

"'Morning, Captain Jack. I'se expecting you might want your gun back. Sorry for borrowing it without asking."

I was dumbfounded and once again tapped my fingers at the place where it should have been.

"How...?" I couldn't find the words.

"It's best if you don't asks no questions you rightly don't want no answers for."

As I took possession of the gun, she seemed to lose her balance a little. "You know, I'se getting to be a little too old to keep saving you."

"You don't have to protect me anymore...the war is over, Vanita."

"Both good and bad for me," she said. "Mister Pickell done run off, and the man who lended him some money on his place done put me out. I studied on doing something to him, but it hardly seems worth the effort. Like I said, I'se getting too old for such things."

I lifted her and put her up on Prize. "You can come with me to Mrs. Jenkins' place. She's a good woman. I'm sure she'll let you stay there with me. You can sleep in Moze's place."

"You'll find she's expecting me."

"What about him?" I asked, pointing at my attacker's body.

"Let's just be on our way. What do you think he'd have done with your body?"

As we reached the streets of town, I thought back to the day we returned to Pickell's farm after visiting Moze. "You know, the word is that Mr. Lincoln freed all the slaves before he died."

"I heard the same thing."

"It's just like you predicted. Years ago, you told me this would happen."

"I didn't predict nothing, boy. I told you then, I done *seen* it, clear as day."

"I don't doubt that you did."

"I got me something else to tell you, Captain Jack. Nobody knows this but me."

"What?"

"When your mama was a-birthin' you, they was some trouble. Your mamma and daddy was staying in Houston at the time. The midwife sent for me. I'd been a midwife for a goodly amount of time, taught most around here that knows the art, both black and white. It was a long spell getting there, but I arrived just in time."

"What do you mean?"

"I saved your mama, but when you was birthed, you warn't breathing, at least not until I blowed a puff of my breath into you. You hacked and coughed something fierce and made the awfulest face I ever seen on a baby, but then you started howling like we'd all been a hoping and expecting. I been watching over you ever since, you just didn't knowed it."

We approached Mrs. Jenkins house, and I lifted Vanita off the saddle. I opened the gate to let Vanita go ahead of me, and I stared at her feeble steps as she walked up the path and marveled at her power.

"Thank you, Captain Jack. I don't reckon I'll be too long of an imposition on you."

Meet Thomas Fenske

Thomas Fenske currently lives in North Carolina but he was born and raised in Texas, and his native Texan roots run deep. He's braved long stretches of endless Texas highways in search of the best Chicken-Fried Steak, Chili, Texas BBQ, and Tex-Mex food. He's hiked west Texas mountains, canoed rapids on the Guadalupe River, suffered through waves of mosquitoes in The Big Thicket, and rafted the Rio Grande. He's blistered in the heat of the long Texas summers, endured hurricanes, ice storms, hail, wind, and floods. He has even ridden across ranchland looking for a lost "little doggie"... how many Texans can say they did that?

Why did he leave the Lone Star State? Well, one must do many strange things to better provide for a family.

He and his lovely wife of thirty-plus years currently share their home with a dog and nine cats. Somehow, he still manages to write amidst the chaos.

Other Works From The Pen

Of Thomas Fenske

The Fever - A riddle, a treasure, and an obsession —how far would you go to feed *your* fever?

A Curse that Bites Deep - Is it truly a curse or is it a homicidal maniac? Wait, could it be both?

Lucky Strike - A decades-old grudge surfaces with a vengeance in a small Texas town, throwing café owner Smidgeon Toll and her boyfriend Sam Milton into a life-or-death struggle against the dark misfortune that threatens their lives.

Visit Our Website

For The Full Inventory
Of Quality Books:

Wings ePress, Inc.
https://wingsepress.com/

Quality trade paperbacks and downloads
in multiple formats,
in genres ranging from light romantic comedy
to general fiction and horror.
Wings has something for every reader's taste.
Visit the website, then bookmark it.
We add new titles each month!

Wings ePress Inc.
3000 N. Rock Road
Newton, KS   67114

Printed in Great Britain
by Amazon